Dancing With Eva

Also by Alan Judd

FICTION

A Breed of Heroes

Short of Glory

The Noonday Devil

Tango

The Devil's Own Work

Legacy

The Kaiser's Last Kiss

NON-FICTION

Ford Madox Ford

The Quest for C: Mansfield Cumming and the Founding
of the Secret Service

First World War Poets (with David Crane)

The Office Life Little Instruction Book (as Holly Budd)

Dancing With Eva

ALAN JUDD

POCKET BOOKS

LONDON • SYDNEY • NEW YORK • TORONTO

First published in Great Britain by Simon & Schuster UK Ltd, 2007
This edition published by Pocket Books, 2008
An imprint of Simon & Schuster UK Ltd
A CBS COMPANY

1 3 5 7 9 10 8 6 4 2

Simon & Schuster UK Ltd
Africa House
64–78 Kingsway
London WC2B 6AH

www.simonsays.co.uk

Simon & Schuster Australia
Sydney

A CIP catalogue record for this book
is available from the British Library

ISBN: 978-1-4165-1114-4

Typeset by M Rules
Printed and bound in Great Britain by
Cox & Wyman Ltd, Reading, Berks

To Richard Holmes, biographer.

Dancing With Eva

ONE

For some weeks Edith left the opened letter on the white mantelpiece in the sitting room. It would have been easy – forefinger and thumb, a flick of the wrist – to consign it to the beech-log fire she always lit in winter just before tea. Then she could have tried to forget it, since he surely would not have written again. If you don't hear from someone for half a century, then suddenly you do, you can assume he's probably not going to pester you for a reply. After all, he couldn't be certain that she was still alive, or well enough to write. Or that she would remember anything of those indistinguishable days and nights of the warm early summer of 1945.

But she left the letter exactly as she had put it down after her first and only reading, neither forgotten nor acknowledged, like the first quiet indication of serious illness. Her

1

housekeeper, Mrs Hoath, would have lifted it to dust each Monday morning, then replaced it with reverential precision. She would have sensed that it was something special because Edith dealt with all other correspondence at the roll-topped desk in William's – her late husband's – study. Mrs Hoath could never have read it, however, even if she had known German. In Germany itself nowadays none of the post-war generation could read Sütterlin, that elaborate old script. The moment she saw the thick black ink with its curves and spikes she was struck by an ancient familiarity, at once intimate and sickening. She was reluctant to read it, even though she did not know whom it was from, but inevitably she did. It had to be from someone of her own generation, what remained of it, the last that was brought up to read and write Sütterlin. When you considered the great writers and thinkers who had used it, as well as the mass of educated people, it was extraordinary that a nation could in two generations render most of its written history inaccessible to itself.

She replied after a long delay, agreeing to receive him. But only this morning, the day of his arrival, did she take up his letter and read it again. She knew what it said, of course, and knew what he wanted, or thought she did. He wanted to see her once more, he said, before they both died. Why, she had thought; what was the point after all this time? Nothing could be undone and now, at their age, there was nothing new to be done. The past was dead and buried, so far as she was concerned.

She wondered, as she put on her reading glasses by the sitting-room window that morning, who had first used that phrase. Shakespeare? Possibly. So much of what the English thoughtlessly said in daily life came from Shakespeare, though typically they didn't know it. They didn't deserve him.

Before allowing the ancient script to claim her again she gazed across the lawn to the dark red Sussex cattle in the field beyond the ha-ha, with the Downs looming behind them. It was a late autumn day of hurrying clouds and gusts that thrashed the clematis against the french windows, spattering raindrops in spiteful bursts that crackled like bullets. Just like bullets. For her that was no offhand expression, no shorthand of the mind. She knew better than most what bullets sounded like, and what they did. It was partly for that reason, and partly because of the myriad other unwanted recollections she had kept out of the light for fifty years, that she was still reluctant to read again what Hans Beck had written.

It was from Munich. He must have returned to his roots, as she so conspicuously had not. Not that there was much left of the old Munich they had known. It had been flattened, blasted and burnt by the British, Canadian and American bombers. Her family's apartment, the block it was

3

in, the entire street had disappeared in a single night towards the end of the war. Luckily, her family was out of it by then, while she herself was safe in the Berghof, the mountain house. She was staying there with her mistress, another Munich girl. The bombers never found it until right at the end, after her mistress and the entourage had left it for good. But during the heavy night raids of that final year they could see the distant red glow in the sky as Munich burned. Hans Beck's home was also destroyed but earlier, she thought. His mother survived but his fourteen-year-old sister – Greta, a pretty dark-haired girl with brown eyes and a ready laugh – was killed. Her body was never found. Caught in the street, escaping the burning building, she had dissolved, a neighbour said, into a mere shower of blood. Edith had not known Hans well then, but later at the Berghof and in Berlin she remembered him mentioning his sister more than men usually did, as if she were his daughter.

His letter recalled another loss, this time an almost complete eclipse, more comprehensive than the loss of buildings or even of thousands of individual lives. It was the loss of a time, a period, a place, of that which appeared to constitute life itself. Perhaps this was inevitable with the passing years and perhaps everyone's youth seemed in later life to have been spent in a different and unrepeatable world. But the busy, retrospective innocence of the period of her own youth was even less repeatable than others. It was not just that the memories of her school, her piano lessons, her gym lessons, her dancing – how she had loved to dance – were remembered only by her, and would die with her; it was that her entire youth, and she herself, would now for all time be seen only in the context of the Armageddon that followed. It was not possible now for anyone to read that she had known Eva Braun, her future employer, simply as the blonde girl, the teacher's daughter, who worked for Hoffmann the photographer, without endowing that insignificant fact with a significance it lacked entirely at the time: that Eva Braun was to become the mistress and, briefly, the wife of Adolf Hitler, the Führer.

Similarly, if they learned that the child Hans Beck had attended the summer camps of the Nazi Party youth wing, they would inevitably see in that a sinister harbinger of the adult. But Hans at that time – she had been mildly interested in him even then – was doing only what other boys did; he wasn't especially Nazi, especially political, especially anything; he was simply there, or thereabouts. Much closer to her life then was Hannah, daughter of the local doctor and her best friend. She had adored Hannah as she had never adored anyone since. Hannah was effortlessly brilliant at everything: her lessons, her gym, her music, her dancing – better than Edith at anything. Edith had envied her without being jealous. She loved and admired her too much for jealousy, loved her wit, her sense of fun, her generosity. When you were with Hannah everything in life seemed more exciting. When you were away from her, you smiled at the thought of her. When Hannah went to America with her family because they were Jewish, and wise or lucky enough to have got out early, Edith didn't ask why it had to be. She didn't generalize from this one instance to countless others, any more than did Hannah. Presented as necessary, it therefore seemed natural, the whole thing, the whole horrible and now incomprehensible thing. It was so big, you didn't see it. 'A crime without a name,' Mr Churchill called it. That was somehow more apt than the name subsequently given to it.

Yet no one now could imagine how you could witness an episode such as Hannah's abrupt flight without questioning its monstrous context. That was the most irretrievable part of that past. It was how one lived then. You did not need to do or be anything; all that was necessary for it to happen was that you did not ask questions. But perhaps not asking questions was still a kind of doing, or being.

Edith crossed the worn Persian carpet to the windows, holding the slightly trembling page into the light. The window pane streamed with rain and the wind chased and flattened the grass on the Downs. She would have the fire lit early, she thought.

In an even, heavy hand, he apologized for surprising her and hoped she was in good health. It had not been easy to establish that she was probably still alive and functioning, nor to discover her married name and address, but the Internet was a great help nowadays. Edith could not imagine how she could feature on the Internet and was impressed that Hans, a man of her own generation, should be so apparently familiar with it. He wrote, he said, because he would like to meet and talk, assuring her he did not seek to resurrect the past, merely to shake hands with it. His letter was frank, reasonable, straightforward, like the man he had appeared to be.

Yet his hand-shaking metaphor was troubling. She imagined actually shaking hands with him again. He would feel like a stranger, surely, despite the fact that they shared memories of great ... great what? Moment? Importance? Historical significance? No, they were too individual, haphazard, ordinary in an everyday sense, for such concepts. Great intensity, then? Days, whole periods of life could be intense without being of lasting importance, even for those involved, even when there were consequences. Perhaps it was the ordinariness that was extraordinary, the daily detail, the mundanity, the watch that ticks indifferently on your wrist throughout the greatest, most terrible events. Perhaps there was significance in that.

But it was not really the thought of an actual handshake that troubled her. It was, as he put it, the handshake with the past that she feared. No matter that there could be few, if any, other survivors of that particular past, of that place and those people. No matter that the fiftieth, then the sixtieth, anniversaries of the ending of the Second World War had been widely recalled and celebrated. No matter that the Nazi-hunters were still in business, tracking down war criminals and making films about them. No matter that perhaps only she and Hans were left alive to say what it was really like in the bunker. For them, there was nothing to be gained from treading that ground again. Only trouble would come of it.

She looked again at the wet cattle intent on their grass, seemingly indifferent to weather. She ought to go to Lewes and shop, but it would be misery. Both driving and walking were a strain in the wet. In her reply to Hans she had suggested he came for tea, and he was due at four. She had no idea where he would travel from. Would tea become dinner? Would he wish to stay the night, or was he booked into an hotel in Lewes? Shelley's, she would have suggested if she had thought. Perhaps they should have met for tea there; it would have kept him and the past at a slightly greater distance.

She lowered the letter and considered her hand, the hand he would expect to shake. She had had fine hands, delicate and shapely; now they were scrawny and bony, like an old chicken's claw, the skin wrinkled and mottled. Were those brown spots – did people call them liver spots? – minor cellular mutations? Were they a sign of cancer, or were they what you got if you hadn't got cancer? William had had almost unblemished skin to the day he died, of cancer. He would have gone to Lewes today, no doubt about it. He enjoyed bad weather and hated shopping, so would try to shop when most people didn't. He conducted shopping expeditions like military operations: identify target, get in and get out as quickly as possible. He was the most equable and peaceful of men, yet the army – at least, the British Army – and the war had suited him well. Despite a comfortable and congenial second career in tea-broking, he probably always thought of himself as essentially the young captain in battledress she had first met near the Rhine in May 1945. If there is a period in life when people are most fully, most completely themselves, then that was his.

It had been a good marriage, on the whole – very good compared with the horror stories she felt she heard daily now – and she sometimes thought that part of the reason was his association of her with the best time of his life. That part of the past had certainly proved benign, and fecund. At least, so far as he was concerned.

Edith folded the letter and walked quickly across the hall to the study. Her steps sounded gratifyingly crisp and purposeful on the parquet hall floor, which smelled pleasantly of Mrs Hoath's polishing. She put the folded letter right at the back of the letter rack as if hiding it, or hiding from it. Despite the solidity and apparent decisiveness of her steps, she felt fragile and threatened. She wanted to say something to Mrs Hoath but for a minute she could not trust herself to speak, and her fingers trembled as she pushed the letter away. It was Michael, her son, whom she felt was threatened by this resurgence of her past. Absurd, of course, because it was nothing to do with him; he had not been born then. He was now a busy and successful commercial barrister, father of her three blessed grandchildren, living not too far away, happily married – so far as one could tell – and well able to look after himself. Hans would never meet him and would never have the opportunity to threaten him, even in the unlikely event that he wanted to; she would see to that. But still she felt the sick panic of imminent discovery, as if she had done something wrong. It was not her fault, none of it was, she told herself.

She went to the kitchen where Mrs Hoath was mashing potatoes in a large bowl. Evidently, Mrs Hoath had decided that the visitor was going to stay to dinner. Edith had told her nothing about him, not even his gender, but Mrs Hoath had a way of sensing things. They had grown old together. Mrs Hoath had started work in the house within a week of William's arrival with his German bride. That was soon enough after the war for there still to be German prisoners-of-war on Home Farm. Edith used to see them in the afternoons as they were driven back to their camp in a slow and wheezy army lorry. They would stare, as they did at any young woman, with a sullen and resentful longing – unlike the Italian POWs who waved and laughed – but she was confident there was nothing about her to show that she was German, and they never heard her speak. Then one day, as she was returning from her walk with Gip, the Jack Russell William had given her, the lorry was even slower than usual, coughing and spluttering as it ground down through the gears almost to a standstill on the narrow S-bend around the churchyard and the shop. She waited for it to pass, holding Gip on his lead, conscious of twenty pairs of eyes searching her from head to toe and careful not to look up, when a voice from above her said, slowly and distinctly, 'Guten Tag, gnadiges Fräulein.'

'Good day, honourable lady.' In English it sounded too contrived, too obviously sarcastic, but in German in those days you could still say it and mean it, which gave the irony its penetrative power. She looked up, unable to stop herself. Twenty young faces, as young as hers, stared down at her with hard and knowing contempt. One – the speaker's she was sure – grinned with presumptuous complicity. 'I know who you are,' his grin said, 'and you know I know, gnadiges Fräulein.'

As soon as the lorry passed she ran up the drive into the manor, lips compressed in the effort to remain dry-eyed. She would have succeeded if she hadn't been caught by Mrs Hoath as she hurried upstairs to her room.

'Excuse me, Mrs Ashburnham, but there is a letter for you.'

It was from Munich, in her mother's writing.

'I thought you was in your room and I was going to bring it up, but here it is.' Mrs Hoath held it out with a smile, pleased because she thought Edith would be pleased.

Edith burst into tears.

It was the start of a state of being later known as depression. She was permanently exhausted, which at the time she attributed to the young Michael, and woke at four every morning with a draining sense of futility and hopelessness. Nothing was worth doing because whatever she did seemed bound to fail, and beneath it all was the debilitating conviction that it wasn't worth it anyway. Everyday actions such as getting up, going out, eating, running a bath, talking, being cheerful – above all sustaining conversation – were achievable, but only with enervating effort. She thought it didn't show but slowly came to suspect that Mrs Hoath understood. Nothing was ever said, of course. It was important that it should not be because what was unspoken was then all the more effective. Numerous little attentions, tiny, unobjectionable sympathies – a cup and saucer moved, flowers placed, tones of voice, the endless help with Michael, blouses and shirts meticulously ironed and folded – made Edith feel that she was liked and looked after. Gradually these little attentions were more restorative than a thousand frank, self-centred conversations. It was then that she and Mrs Hoath formed the bond that was to endure life-long, not only because of Edith's debilitation and Mrs Hoath's kindness, but because they were both having to cope with Dorothy, William's mother.

Formidable and direct, Dorothy was loyal to the values of her youth, which were really those of the generation before her own. She was busy, intelligent, with little imagination and no more intellectual curiosity than was necessary to cope with the world in which she found herself, but she had a ready practical sympathy once she perceived that sympathy was needed, and merited. She had not been pleased when her only son had brought home a German bride. 'I think we have had enough of Germans for a while, they should make themselves scarce for the next half century,' she said to the rector when he urged reconciliation and rejoicing. But she determined to make the best of what at first she regarded as a bad job, and kept her feelings largely to herself. When the job turned out to be not at all bad – as she later put it to Edith – she admitted that even at the time she thought it could have been worse. Better that William should have come home from the war with a charming and well-intentioned German addition to himself, rather than with bits of his body or mind missing, or with an unwelcome addition such as some dreadful English flapper he had picked up in London or somewhere, as some of his regimental colleagues had done.

But Edith's state of near-collapse passed Dorothy by. She noticed that the girl seemed always tired but put it down to the baby and the poor diet of wartime Germany, the latter with the clear implication that it was their own fault. In fact, Edith's diet in the Führer's court had been excellent, probably superior to any to be had in Britain. Certainly superior to anything enjoyed by her family and friends in Munich. She had been aware of that at the time and had felt guilty. Later it was both reassuring and disconcerting to recall that she was, therefore, capable of guilt.

Fortunately, Dorothy's attention was diverted by her growing grandchild and by having a new housekeeper to break in, as she put it. Apart from having to be broken in, Mrs Hoath anyway had ground to make up. A village girl of good repute, she had made, in Dorothy's view, a hasty wartime marriage to a man from Brighton. While not disapproving of hasty marriages – her own son's, after all, had been even more rapid – Dorothy did not approve of men from Brighton. Yet Mr Hoath, a self-employed bricklayer, appeared to be neither idle nor a ruffian nor a drunk. He improved the cottage that went with his wife's job at the manor and over the years made himself useful in many other ways. As Dorothy could no longer afford to staff the manor as it had been in her late husband's time – there were three Mrs Hoaths before the war, as well as various outside men – she came gradually to appreciate Mr Hoath's solid virtues. She nevertheless confessed to Edith that she always feared that if 'anything happened' Mr Hoath would be in danger of 'reverting to type'.

William, more intuitive than his mother, had been considerate and attentive, aware that something was wrong. Edith encouraged his inclination to attribute her lassitude to the baby and to post-war exhaustion, from which many people suffered. Her sudden descent into deep wells of depression – bottomless black pits from which, when in them, it was impossible to conceive release – he put down to the pressures and compromises forced upon any decent personality within the circle of the late Führer. There was perhaps some truth in that, and she was content for him to assume it, although it was only half true at best. But his very consideration made her feel worse and his tenderness was at times unendurable. She baffled and disappointed him, yet he was uncomplaining, confident that she would eventually come out of it. Gradually she did, as Michael grew and the future reasserted itself.

Michael was destined to be an only child whereas Mrs Hoath went on to produce three in almost indecently quick succession. Dorothy had to take on extra help but permitted Mrs Hoath to bring her brood to work with her, penned into the nursery with Michael. Edith and Mrs Hoath became close during those early years, while maintaining the formality of address that Dorothy took so completely for granted. Mrs Hoath was never Eileen, Dorothy was always ma'am and Edith Mrs Ashburnham while Dorothy lived, and ma'am thereafter. It could have changed after Dorothy's death and Edith made tentative opening remarks in that direction, but Mrs Hoath, perhaps fearing it might be the harbinger of other, less welcome changes, said promptly that ma'am had been so right for the old Mrs Ashburnham that it would dishonour her memory to abandon it with the new. Edith, still ignorant of changing British mores, allowed it to continue.

Now Mrs Hoath was a grey-haired old lady, like Edith only stouter, with a red, round, wrinkled face and worn but capable old hands. She mashed the potatoes with practised ease and economy of effort, necessary now that her breathing was so laboured. She wore a pink and white flowered apron, the latest of a line that went back over half a century. She wore soft old slippers for her bunions. Dorothy would never have permitted slippers, Edith reflected inconsequentially as she hesitated over what to say to Mrs Hoath. Dorothy disliked slippers on anyone anywhere, except in the bathroom and bedroom. They made people sloppy, she said.

'I just thought in case he might be staying to dinner,'

ma'am,' Mrs Hoath said while Edith was still forming her words.

'Yes, thank you. It is possible he might.' She had not said that the guest was a man, but Mrs Hoath knew.

'Will the gentleman be staying the night, ma'am?'

'No. Unless he asks. I suppose he could if he wishes. But there has been no mention of it. I haven't invited him.'

'Only I've made the bed up in the front guest room, just in case.'

'Thank you.'

Edith's panic subsided in the presence of Mrs Hoath but left her still impatient to be doing and saying. She clasped her hands and looked again at their mottled skin. 'I'm worried about the flower show.'

Mrs Hoath added milk and butter to the potatoes.

Edith continued: 'One reads of so many break-ins these days. Every week there is another. Jane Oxley – you know, the retired teacher who's moved in next door to the old post office and is now our new neighbourhood watch co-ordinator – was saying that the police think the thieves use open garden days to reconnoitre houses. Well, of course, at the flower show every year there are masses of people here we don't know. It's a perfect opportunity for them to look over the place, even when they are not allowed in. And, of course, there's only me now. I couldn't do much to stop them. I'm not even sure where the keys to William's gun cabinet are.'

Mrs Hoath transferred the mashed potatoes to the large dish of cooked mutton, deftly smoothing them with an old broad-bladed knife. Famed at the monthly village market for her pies, she had fewer opportunities to show off with just Edith to cook for.

'People say it's the gyppos. Always more crime when they are in the area. But the flower show has always been here, longer than anyone can remember.'

'Yes, I know, I know.'

Clasping and unclasping her hands, Edith went to the telephone on the hall table, closing the kitchen door behind her. She was oppressed again by the unasked question of when she should hand over the manor to Michael and his family and move herself into one of the cottages. Probably the stone one by the old school house where generations of Home Farm shepherds had lived. She had always liked that, particularly the garden and the fact that it was just across the road from the church. The question remained unasked because of her anxiety as to whether her daughter-in-law, Sarah, would actually want the manor. She had made no hints, shown no sign of that interest in a house which a woman who has it cannot help betraying. Either she was being very tactful and circumspect or she really did not want the crumbling old place, with its ancient wiring, idiosyncratic plumbing and rotting window frames. She had a taste for the modern, Sarah, or at least for the efficient. There was nothing sentimental about her. It was a reversal of national stereotypes: Sarah as the modern, clinically efficient German woman, herself as the quaint and sentimental Englishwoman. She would have to speak frankly to Michael; that was the only way.

She was aware of the unreason of her action as she dialled Sarah's number on the heavy black phone in the hall, but it didn't stop her. Sarah answered, sounding harassed, the noise of the children in the background. She was always friendly enough but the briskness of her manner unnerved Edith, making her feel she was intruding. Clearly, Sarah was anxious for her mother-in-law to come to the point and say why she was ringing. Edith felt her panic return, gripping her from within like some dreadful paralysing disease. She couldn't say what she was ringing about, not because she couldn't bring herself to say it but because its origin was fear, fear of age, fear of loneliness, fear of death, as well as a more irrational fear for Michael and the children. She again felt that Michael was in some way under threat, and that she was responsible. She rang off after saying she could hear that Sarah must be busy and would speak to her later. There was relief and puzzlement in Sarah's goodbye; Edith imagined her later saying something to Michael about his mother's odd behaviour. When she put the phone down her skin was prickling with discomfort.

She sought relief in the music room, at her piano. The

impersonal absorption in technique and the attempt to give voice to emotions as full as the sea was preferable to human contact. The room was cold and the piano lid heavy. It was too long since she had practised. She chose Schubert's evocative song 'Der Vollmond Straht', a tale of love denied and of both hearts breaking, a difficult, haunting and elusive piece. She felt she was forever approaching its essence and never reaching it. It was like the scent of bluebells in a wood, enticing, tantalizing but ultimately uncapturable. For a while, her efforts to achieve what Schubert offered absorbed her entirely.

TWO

He arrived promptly at four. In fact, a minute early, a mark perhaps of his military youth. 'If you are on time, you are late,' William had been fond of saying, adding that it was a piece of British Army doctrine he had been unable to take off with his uniform. Perhaps it had been the same for Hans in the German Army.

He arrived in a Lewes hire car, carrying a substantial brown briefcase that could just serve as an overnight bag. His long coat emphasized his height. She had forgotten how tall he was; the Führer, who was quite short, liked to have tall men about him. Hans stood hatless and unhurried in the rain, looking at her. What was left of his hair was silver now. Its thinning made his features, especially his nose, more prominent than she remembered. He was much wrinkled, of course, and his cheeks were sunken. As he walked towards her across the gravel she reflected that she might have passed him in the street without knowing him. He was probably thinking the same of her.

He approached with a slightly rueful smile, the smile of a little boy who knows he has done wrong, but not too badly wrong, and is hopeful of forgiveness. He stopped at the foot of the steps, still heedless of the rain.

'Edith, I have only one question to ask. And perhaps you have one of me. It is not necessary to come in if you prefer that I do not.'

Then why have you come? she thought. You could have asked your question by letter. 'Don't be ridiculous, Hans, of course you must come in. I have tea ready.'

They sat in the sitting room on either side of the fire, the tea tray on the low table between them. Though stiff in his movements, he appeared physically relaxed, yet his carefully chosen phrases and tentative delivery made her wonder whether he was in fact as nervous as herself. He seemed wary.

She poured from Dorothy's battered silver teapot. He looked around the room. 'So, Edith, how did you come here?'

In the mouth of a native English speaker it might have sounded insolent, but in German it was matter-of-fact. He spoke the old German, the German of her youth. She was silenced, temporarily disarmed. It was the same question, the very same words that her husband had asked her in the first minute of their first meeting. And then, as now, she hesitated.

That was within days of the end of the war during her initial interrogation in the patched-up office of a bombed munitions factory that the British had renamed Interrogation Centre, Holding Camp 106. It was shortly after she had escaped Berlin and at first she felt resentful and unlucky at having been picked up by the British. Many thousands wandered Germany at that time, trying to get home, like her, or trying to get anywhere or nowhere, or just trying to keep going. Most were of no interest to the occupying armies but she had been stopped by soldiers at a checkpoint at the entrance to a village. After asking where she had come from and hearing her cautious English, they talked amongst themselves and then firmly helped her – she was very weak – into the back of their lorry.

She had hesitated over his first question, not because she was trying to decide whether to tell her interrogator the truth – she had at that stage no thought of lying and was anyway too exhausted to invent. What made her hesitate was the young captain's German, grammatically correct and unsurprisingly spoken with an English accent, but lacking conviction. He spoke as if he didn't really mean what he said, or didn't believe he could really say it. William had never managed to sound convincing in German, always too diffident, too tentative, yet always correct. On that first occasion she paused because she was trying to decide whether to appear helpful by using her English. It was by no means fluent and, apart from the few words exchanged with the soldiers, she had not used it since school, where she had been a diligent student.

'I walked,' she replied in German.

'From where?'

'Berlin.'

'Alone?'

'Some of the time with another woman, called Heidi. I never knew her other name. She was also trying to get to Munich.'

'For how many days have you walked?'

His manner was sympathetic, as if he trusted her. Her worn and filthy shoes should have been evidence enough, though she herself was thankfully clean at last. Imprisonment had been an unexpected relief because the English soldiers had got the factory shower working and for the first time in days – weeks? – she had washed herself thoroughly. And she had been fed. But she still wore the hateful, dirty and ill-fitting woollen shirt she had found in a barn, and the ragged jersey and oversized, high-shouldered coat she had acquired during the escape from Berlin. It had been welcome at the time; anything to get out of the clothes she was wearing.

'More than four days,' she replied. 'I'm not sure. Sometimes at night as well, so I have lost count. It depends which day it is now. I think I left during the night of May the second. Probably, something like that.'

'Eight days, then.'

He smiled. It was the first time anyone had smiled at her since – she tried to think – since Eva Braun, just before she died. 'Give Bavaria my love,' she had said. 'Maybe you will see it again, I shall not.' Edith had seen that smile through her own tears, at once reluctant and genuine. She almost wept now at this young English officer's small, rather shy smile. He was looking across his desk at her shoes, her feet, her legs. She wanted to hide herself and longed for decent clothes again. Even the wooden chair she sat on was old and rickety, good only for firewood. The sun broke through the patched-up window behind him, lightening his fair hair and picking out the captain's pips on the epaulettes of his brown battledress tunic. The shoulder flashes announced him as Intelligence Corps. From outside there was shouting and the sounds of lorries.

'What did you eat?' he asked.

'Anything we could find in the fields. Berries. Potatoes when it was possible to boil them. Sometimes bread when I still had things to barter. Once we had cheese and sausages at a farm, when I was still with Heidi. They gave them to us.' It was an inexpressible relief to have been fed after her capture, to know there would be more food and that she was safe. It made her want to talk now.

'What happened to Heidi?'

'She went off with some other people we met who said they knew how to get to the Americans.'

'You didn't go with them?'

'I was too tired. My feet were bleeding. I fell asleep in a barn. She said she would come back if she found the Americans. I never saw her after that.'

He had her identity card before him. 'You were a secretary in the Reich Chancellery?'

'Yes.'

'Whom did you work for?'

'Various officers.' She felt the change in her tone and, from his pause, suspected he had noticed. He did not hurry to continue, as if to let her know that he knew.

'Anyone in particular?'

It was the moment she had known would come sometime but she had done nothing to prepare for it. She should have thought about it but other things were more immediate – hunger, thirst, fear, weariness. And other things.

'I worked for Fraulein Braun.'

'Who was she?'

'The Führer's – Herr Hitler's – mistress.'

'Not his housekeeper?'

She shrugged. 'Well, she didn't have any duties like that.

He had housekeepers. He married her, at the end.'

'Frau Hitler, then. That sounds strange.' He smiled again.

'It did to him, too. He still referred to her as Fraulein Braun. And to her. She almost signed herself as that on the marriage certificate.'

'Do you know what happened to Hitler?' His tone was very gentle.

She was surprised. 'He killed himself. Didn't you know? And she. They are both dead.'

'Are you sure? Did you see them? Tell me what happened.'

It was impossible to tell it all because she had remembered too much, too many details, a surfeit of unwanted impressions, incidentals, sounds, smells. Later it was impossible because she had forgotten too much, and remembered only what she had said before. This time, the first of many times she had to tell it, she described only events, the bare factual account. He took notes.

Even so, her own words started up flocks of memories in her head, wheeling, re-forming and scattering like starlings. But already she was discarding and selecting, pushing aside those thousand felt incidentals that narrative squeezed out. They were not essential to events yet they were the context out of which events were formed. How could you account for what the Führer did, for the power he had, without knowing what it felt like to be in his presence? His blue

27

eyes, so very blue, so filled with emotion and conviction that your own arguments, if you had any, were not so much overthrown as not even formulated, not even capable of formulation, in his presence. His will did not so much dominate as exclude all others and it was only afterwards, when you left the presence, that your own thoughts crept back through you, like blood returning to a numbed limb. His want was like a child's want, an all-consuming ache that demanded assuagement. Yet what evoked this most strongly for Edith, as she constructed the fixed narrative she would repeat many times over the years, was something that had nothing to do with anything the Führer did himself. In those last minutes of his and Eva's lives, as he said farewell outside his room deep in the bunker, by then fetid with diesel, stale air, sweat, cooking, urine and petrol stacked in jerry cans for his funeral pyre, he was not a force but a wreck, a hunched, shaking, almost voiceless husk of a man. It smelt of him, too, of his appalling halitosis that lately gusted from him when he spoke to you. Even at this climactic moment of their lives – and of everyone else's, for they all knew that this was the end – Edith could not help wondering how Eva bore his halitosis, and whether – as his wife now – she would say anything about it.

But it was Eva herself who most vividly conveyed the power that Hitler had been. Eva smiling through moist eyes, resplendent in the Italian black silk dress with pink shoulder straps, black suede shoes with fashionable cork heels, pearl necklace, gold clip in her tinted blonde hair and the platinum watch with diamond numbers that he had given her. That this vigorous thirty-three-year-old woman, who did not want to die, whom Edith had loved and hated and who at her end could say, with a sad smile, that she was determined to be a pretty corpse – that this creature so obviously full of life and warm blood, could die with this stinking, morose, mumbling wreck – that was what spoke to Edith of his power. But it was no part of the narrative.

Yet even then somehow, against their wills, he held them. He shook hands with the women only, his hand limp and already almost inert, as he muttered soft farewells. He still had that Austrian charm, artificial, meaningless, irresistible. And Edith, her own eyes by then full of tears, still adored, still hated Eva as she retreated into Hitler's room with him and turned in the door, the last she would ever pass through. She smiled at Edith, mouthed farewell and held up her hand.

But the British Army wanted none of this. Her interrogator was more interested in the dead.

'How did Hitler die?'

'He shot himself.'

'Did you see or hear him do it?'

'No. He was in his rooms, alone with Eva. The heavy outer door was closed. Otto Günsche, his adjutant, stood before it holding his pistol across his chest.'

'But did you hear the shot?'

'No, I had gone upstairs with Traudl Junge, one of his sec-retaries, to the room where the six Goebbels children were. We sang songs with them, the children were doing part-singing.'

'What happened to those children?'

'Their mother killed them.'

'So the singing would have drowned out the shot?'

'Not only the singing. There were explosions, shells falling, in the Chancellery garden. Upstairs there was the noise of the generators. Also Hitler's rooms were some dis-tance below and they were behind two doors, the outer one very heavy.'

'Did you actually see Hitler's dead body?'

'Yes.'

Edith paused. He was noting everything now and she felt suddenly weary, as if a trapdoor had opened inside her and drained all her energy. He probably interpreted her pause as indicating emotion or difficulty of some sort, something significant. But it was nothing of the kind. What she had seen simply had no interest for her now. It hadn't even at the time. It was over, all of it, the past was past, the future unknowable, not even interesting. The bodies were merely the sweepings of history. And the more important the details seemed to her interrogator, the more distant she felt from them and him.

'Where did you see the body?'

'In his living room, where he died. Eva's body was there too.'

'Describe it. Describe exactly where Hitler's body was.'

He was plainly not interested in Eva.

Edith described what she had seen when she went in behind Günsche. Bormann, the Führer's evil genius whom everyone hated – none more than Eva – was already there with Linge, the ever-faithful valet. She described the scene with weary matter-of-factness, as if for the hundredth time and without suspecting that she would indeed have to describe it a hundred times.

The bodies were on the blue and white striped sofa opposite the door. The Führer was seated on the left side as you looked, his feet on the floor, his head tilted to the right and his right hand resting open on his right thigh, palm upward. There was a dark, round wound in his right temple about the size of an old three-mark piece and a streak of blood on his cheek. To the left of the sofa, beneath his head, there was a puddle of blood on the carpet about the size of a dinner plate. There were spatterings of blood on the sofa and on the wall. A pistol lay on the floor by his feet. He always carried a pistol. His eyes were open. There was a very strong smell of almonds.

'What was he wearing?'

'The almond smell was from the poison pills, the suicide pills, that Himmler had provided and that we were all issued with. That is how Eva killed herself. The Führer was wearing his usual clothes – uniform jacket, black trousers, black socks, black gloves. He had his gloves on but no hat.'

'What became of Himmler?'

'I don't know. He wasn't with us in the bunker.'

'Hitler was definitely dead?'

'Of course. And Eva. She was sitting at the other end of the sofa with her legs drawn up and pointed to her left, away from the Führer. Her hands were clasped in her lap. Her head was upright and her eyes open and her mouth closed. She was looking straight at us, unchanged from when I had seen her ten minutes before. There was no blood and no marks.'

'What happened to Hitler's body?'

'She had taken off her shoes before putting her feet on the sofa. Her shoes were arranged neatly, side by side on the floor, pointing towards us. That was typical of her.'

He put down his pencil and looked at her. His hair was more sandy than fair and she noticed his freckles for the first time. He was not far from her own age, a few years older, probably in his middle or late twenties. She expected him to be sharp, to tell her to answer the questions and not to keep on about Eva. Instead he said quietly, 'Were you fond of Eva Braun?'

This was the only difficult question she was asked. She liked him for asking it, grateful because he seemed interested and it was not just something else for his notebook. She strove to answer accurately. 'I was at first fond of her and liked her and admired her very much. Then I liked her less and did not admire her. But at the end I felt for her.'

He picked up his pencil again. He was left handed. 'Did you see what happened to both their bodies?' He emphasized 'both' very slightly.

'I saw them on the stairs later. Günsche and Linge or maybe Kempka, the Führer's driver, carried his body under a blanket. I saw his black socks and shoes sticking out. And Bormann carried Fräulein Braun – Frau Hitler – over his shoulder, like a sack, at least part of the way. Yes, Bormann,' she added, more to herself than to him. Bormann, loathed Bormann, on whose arm Eva had so often to walk into dinner at the Berghof forcing herself to smile and to endure his own smiling taunts. 'Then Bormann must have handed her over to Günsche because he told me about it afterwards.'

'What happened to Bormann?'

'He escaped with the rest of us. Later, in the streets, he and some others tried to get across a bridge behind a German tank but the Russians blew up the tank and Bormann was knocked over. I never saw him after that.'

'What did Günsche tell you about the disposal of the bodies?'

'He came back into the bunker and sat next to me in the room where I was sitting with Traudl Junge. We were

ALAN JUDD

wondering what we should do now and smoking our cigarettes. We could smoke, you see, because now the Führer was dead. Günsche was pale and looked shocked. He said, "Now I have completed the last and most difficult order of my life. I have burnt the Chief and Eva. Eva was warm when I carried her up. But the poison smells terribly of almonds, I cannot endure this smell any more." They were burned with the petrol from the jerry cans that Kempka had provided.'

'Did you see the bodies burning?'

'Yes. A short while later I climbed the stairs and looked out into the garden. It was not safe to go out because shells were falling and there were bullets. The Russians were very close but I don't think they realized the significance of this place. It looked like a battlefield, all churned up. And there must have been many other bodies there. Fegelein's, for one.'

'Spelt?'

She spelt Fegelein for him, adding, 'He was the SS liaison officer, liaising between Himmler and Hitler. He was one of Himmler's favourites and was quite close to Eva. Hitler had him shot.'

He noted diligently. 'But you definitely saw Hitler's and Eva's bodies burning?'

'I did not go right out but they were not far from the bunker entrance, in a dip in the ground.'

'What did you see?'

34

'A lot of smoke and flames. It was very hot. You could feel it.'

'Could you smell anything?'

'Petrol and roast pork.'

'Could you see the actual bodies? Were you certain it was them?'

'I could not see their heads or the upper parts because of the flames, although at one moment the wind blew the flames and I did see the Führer's head, which was split open on one side. He was on his back, his knees raised and his shin bones showing white but his shoes and socks were unburnt. Eva was lying face down. You could tell by her stockinged feet.'

'What time did all this happen?'

'The time?' That was difficult. The bunker had its own time, with no distinction between night and day. The Führer was nocturnal and their world was imploding. It was possible to describe but impossible to convey the simultaneous intensity and lassitude of life there. There was intensity because of what was happening and because the presence of the Führer made everything intense; there was lassitude because they were all exhausted and knew, but dared not say, that there was no hope. There was a sense that everything that mattered had happened already, or – for some – was still to come; but then, in that very present, nothing mattered. There was nowhere to go, nothing to do.

'I don't know the actual time. It was during the afternoon. We had had lunch.' The Führer had been relaxed and cheerful over lunch, with no mention of suicide.

'On the thirtieth of April?'

It was hard to satisfy his insistence on dates. She nodded and said something, without knowing what. William, as she later came to know him, smiled and put down his pencil again. 'You are tired, Fräulein. You will remember more clearly with more sleep and more food. Thank you for your help. There is only one more question now: I must ask you to submit to having your photograph taken.'

She still had that photograph somewhere. William kept a copy, she had discovered later. It showed a pale nervous young woman with wide staring eyes, her hair longer than she would later wear it and already in need of another wash. She looked lost in that huge high-shouldered coat.

THREE

That was pretty much how Hans would have seen her last, she reflected as she sipped her tea. In that very coat. Perhaps she should show it to him and see how he reacted.

She repeated his question. 'How did I come here? I married my interrogator.'

'A novel method of resistance to interrogation.'

'There was no method. It was not really an interrogation, more an interview. He was mainly interested in the chronology of what had happened to members of the High Command. I told him as best I could. Then I was asked to help with some interpreting, although my English wasn't very good. Then they found me accommodation of my own and paid me. They made a job for me. They treated me well. In the course of my work I had frequent contact with William. We grew to like each other, despite the British no-frat rules. That meant "no fraternization".'

He nodded and smiled as though it were all predictable.

'And you?' she asked. 'How did you get here?'

'Sadly, none of my interrogators proposed marriage. Perhaps because I spoke no Russian.' He smiled again, but slightly. 'I was released in 1953 after eight years. They were not good years. We were badly treated. At first, in the Moscow prison, they appeared not to believe that Hitler was dead, thinking he had been spirited away to South America or somewhere by the imperialist capitalist West with which we were all in league. Of course, we now know that the Russian leadership knew all along that he was dead. They had his remains – but they preferred to accuse the West of fascist sympathies and to beat us because we could not prove he was dead. It was what would nowadays be termed torture. Then afterwards in the labour camp it was hard. Many died. I was ill when I was released and spent a long time in hospital. After that I worked for a firm of building surveyors and in my spare time studied to become one. I qualified and married. We had no children and my wife is dead.'

His account stopped short of the explanation Edith wanted but was reluctant to request outright. After all, he had taken the initiative and so it was for him to explain himself. But life was too short now, she decided, to wait upon proprieties that no one else seemed to notice.

'So why have you come here?' she asked.

He shrugged. 'We are near the ends of our lives, Edith. My

asthma seems to be getting worse, making everything more difficult, and I want to find out what happened to everyone else who was there while I still can. I visited Traudl Junge and Otto Günsche before they died. Some of us I was not able to find before they died. Are you simply not interested in what happened to us all?'

'For me we were never us.' Her own words surprised her. Speaking again in German was unfamiliar and liberating.

His condescending smile further irritated her. He would not be staying to dinner, let alone for the night. He was, and was not, the Hans she had known. Physically, he appeared to become more recognizable as she became used to him; she hoped – almost despite herself – that it was the same with her. But the young Hans had been easy-going, charming, likeable, untrustworthy and dislikeable only at the end. His blue eyes had attracted her. They were almost as blue as the Führer's but friendlier and more humorous; cheating blue eyes, it turned out. They were paler and greyer now, behind the severe steel-framed glasses, and he seemed to have lost his desire, or need, to charm. His manner was harder and less considerate than it used to be. He made no attempt at sympathy but appeared to assume a superior understanding, as if she were a beginner on a journey and he an experienced traveller. She would probably not even offer to refill the teapot, she thought.

'True, we are no longer us,' he said. 'Not now nor at any

time since. It became necessary not to be us in order to survive. But then, in that bunker, we were us. And the world regards us still as "them" – regardless of our feelings about it, of our differences and of the accidents that brought us together. And if the world sees you as a group, you are one. In all things the world's view, however wrong or oversimplified, predominates. The only way to recover one's individuality is to remember. Memory, no matter how false and unreliable, no matter that it is so often a construct to sustain our contemporary survival, is the only key to what we really are. Or rather, the only way of establishing whether we really are anything at all.' He put down his cup. 'I suspect that for you, Edith, the past is water under the bridge. That is what you would say, yes?'

'Yes.'

'It is understandable. It is how very many people sustained their lives, and for that reason alone one should not criticize it. Life is worth sustaining and if the price is a necessary myth or exclusion of significant events or periods, then so be it. The present matters because it is becoming the past and the past is what we are. The future is unknowable, unpredictable, therefore of no account. But for me it is impossible to see the past as you do, as water under the bridge. We are the sum of our pasts. The past is the only way by which the present may be understood. Why seek to understand the present, you may ask. Indeed. Millions live their lives without ever seeking understanding of themselves. They may be wise. Or, more likely, it is not a choice; they are unaware of their uninterest and so are not unhappy. Or not unhappy about that. But if you are different, then you cannot be uninterested in how you came here, wherever here is, and that means being interested in the past, however patchy, unreliable or unreclaimable that past is.'

'There is a novel, an English novel,' she said, 'the first line of which is: "The past is another country: they do things differently there."'

'Yes, I know that novel. I read it because I heard of that beginning.' When he nodded the fire danced in his glasses, giving him the momentary appearance of a symbolist painting or of a soul in torment. 'I imagine that novel as having taken place in a beautiful old English house such as this.'

'Grander than this, I think.'

'It is a wonderful beginning, but, like so many memorable quotations, wonderful but wrong. Or neither right nor wrong. We nod our heads in uncritical acceptance but we do not examine it. In one sense it is right: the past is another country because the conditions of life were different then. They always were. But we were not, we were not different. It is wrong to suggest that we were by saying, "They do things differently there." They did as we would have under those conditions. We are as they were. They were us. That is why we can understand them, but we can do so only in so far as we are able to understand how our own pasts have made us what we are. The understanding of our own pasts is essential to the understanding of the past in general. That is why, Edith, I am so interested in the last ten days in the Führerbunker.'

'I don't see how raking over all that again would tell us anything we don't already know about those times and those people. Or ourselves.'

He made a movement that was not quite a gesture, a shift in his armchair that ended with his re-crossing his legs and glancing at the windows as another gust of rain rattled them. She noticed they were leaking again, letting water in at the bottom. There was discoloration of the floorboards. It used to happen whenever the rain came strongly from the south-west, and Mr Hoath had repaired them once. She would mention it to Mrs Hoath.

'Perhaps it wouldn't tell us anything we don't know,' he said. 'Perhaps we know enough. But it might help us to understand better. We still don't understand, neither what we ourselves did, nor what we all did.'

'But we didn't all do it.'

His tufty white eyebrows showed briefly above his glasses 'Did we not?'

The door opened and Mrs Hoath entered slowly with the big black kettle. 'I'm just off now, ma'am. Everything's done and just needs heating up when you're ready.'

Hans stood as if for a guest. Edith just stopped herself replying in German. 'Thank you, Mrs Hoath. That will be excellent.'

'And I thought the pot might be ready for a top-up.'

'Thank you.'

Hans smiled at Mrs Hoath in mock complicity. 'You know the secret of good tea, Mrs Hoath.'

'Thank you, sir.'

He sat while she carefully filled the teapot. 'I see the rain's coming under them doors again,' she said to Edith.

'I'm afraid so.'

'I'd better tell Jack about it.'

'There's no hurry. There's not much.'

Mrs Hoath closed the door after another exchange of smiles with Hans. She was probably impressed by his manners and his remembering her name. Edith moved the teapot to the hearth. 'I take it you would you like more tea?'

'Thank you.'

She was no longer so annoyed with him. His evident seriousness endeared him a little, whether or not she agreed with what he said. 'What exactly is it that you wish to understand?'

'You were with Eva long before the bunker. I can't remember that you ever told me how you got your job.'

This too echoed her early sessions with William. 'I wanted to be a dancer.' She smiled now at the thought. 'I was very keen but my parents were very opposed, especially my mother, who said that no good ever came of Munich girls who went off to Berlin. We had great arguments about it. Of course, I would never have succeeded; I wasn't good enough but I didn't know that then. I almost didn't care, anyway, so determined was I to oppose my mother. I had two friends who had gone to Berlin and they said they would find me a job if I joined them in their flat and helped to pay the rent. That is what happened. At first I was a clerk in an insurance company and then I was a secretary for a shoe manufacturer. Somehow I assumed that, just by being in Berlin, I would become a dancer. You remember how some young men used to spend all their time and money in certain cafés, thinking that was how to become a poet or an artist? Perhaps you do not. Perhaps those were not your circles. Fortunately for me, the war changed things so much, with so many dance schools and theatres closing, that I had no chance to discover that I was not capable of becoming a dancer.

'I met Eva – Fräulein Braun, Frau Hitler – because she had shoes made especially for her by our company. She was very serious about shoes, serious about all clothes. Sometimes when she was in Berlin she would come to our offices to discuss new shoes with the owner and the designer. I would make coffee for everybody. Of course, she took no notice of me until my employer made a joke one day about how the company always preferred to deal with ladies from Bavaria and told her where I was from. I knew who she was but I had never said. When she realized that I was almost a neighbour of hers in Munich, that I knew where she lived, knew her by sight, she was friendly to me and after that always said a few words.

'Of course, we never knew who she was actually with then. That is, what she actually was. Nobody did. She was a state secret, as you know. Her bills were settled by the Reich Chancellery. We just assumed she had some important role there, or some important Party connection. We did not ask questions. People didn't then. We would never have dreamed that she was the Führer's mistress, or even that he had one – if he really did, but that's another question that some people worry about. I don't. And if we had dreamt it, we should never have said anything. People didn't then. That was one of many ways in which that past was really another country.'

Edith took the teapot from the hearth and poured, a little amused by her own loquacity. Well, if he wanted to hear about such things, he could. Not many people did, when it came to it. Most were more interested in their own concerns or their own histories than in anything anyone else said about themselves. It was the same in nearly all conversations: while someone was telling you something you often couldn't wait for them to pause because of what you wanted to tell them. You had only to eavesdrop on other people's conversations to hear it happening. That was why conversation was so rarely sequential; people announced more than they answered. But if Hans became awkward or too pressing, she knew she had questions that would stop him in his tracks. And he would know that she had.

She handed him his tea. 'Then one day my boss came to me and said, "Fräulein Braun would like you to work for her. She wishes you to go for an interview. Here is the address." When I asked what she did and what she wanted me to do, he just shrugged. He seemed sad that I might leave but acted as if it was inevitable. He was a nice man but I was happy to leave because the job was really very boring and I wanted to change. All my life I had loved to change. I didn't like to do anything for long. And Fräulein Braun was very pretty and always beautifully dressed and obviously rich and well connected. Everything about her seemed glamorous and I felt flattered that she had chosen me, no matter what for. In fact, I think it really didn't matter what for, so long as I was a success at it, I didn't ask more than that. The only thing that troubled me was the address: it was the Berghof, of course, where she lived, but I didn't know that then. All I knew was that I had to go all the way to Austria, to a mountain village to which I had never heard of called Berchtesgaden, near Salzburg. With the address were train tickets so I would not have to pay, so that was all right. Also, the journey would take me through Munich, so I could stop off and see my family, which was more than all right. Although I was living in Berlin against their wishes and determined to go on doing so, I did of course miss them very much. I think I would have gone for the interview even if I hadn't wanted the job, just for the chance to spend a night in Munich.

'The trains were still running then, although there were many delays because of the bombing. When I reached Munich I was shocked. There was so much destruction, so many homeless people, people with nothing at all. Not only houses and flats had disappeared but whole streets were rubble and over everything there was always this horrible smell of burning and dust and sewage. Of course, I had seen some of that in Berlin and even worse later, but at that stage of the war Berlin was better defended and anyway it was bigger. Fortunately my family's apartment was still all right and they were well. I stayed the night, which was a surprise for them, especially as I had brought some food. They were hungry, of course, although not as hungry as later. Your family's street, too, was still untouched and your sister . . .'

She hesitated, fearing she should not have mentioned it, but his face betrayed nothing. He continued to stare at her with an expression of intelligent inquiry, like a consultant physician listening to an account of symptoms. She wanted to ask if he had discovered where little Greta was buried but thought better of it. Probably a mass grave somewhere.

'The Führer never saw any of that,' she continued. 'He never visited bombed areas like the English king and queen or Mr Churchill. He travelled from headquarters to headquarters in his special train, usually at night and always with the blinds down, even in daylight. He never liked the light. He said it was harmful for his blue eyes. And if he had to go into the sun he always wore a hat, especially at the Berghof where there was so much snow to dazzle him. But he rarely went into the sun, anyway. I think it was not just his eyes. He disliked the sun. He always avoided the light.'

'You are suggesting this was the physical manifestation of a spiritual condition?'

'Perhaps you could see it like that. I was met at the station by a black car with two SS men. Nothing like that had ever happened to me before. I was frightened. It was as if I was being arrested. We drove a long way and finally up the mountain road to the Berghof and they talked as if there was no one with them, ignoring me entirely. I didn't know what they thought I was. Later, I realized they probably thought I was one of the prostitutes ordered up sometimes for the SS house staff and guards. And for officers as well, for all I know. But if they had thought that, they might have been friendlier. I became even more nervous.

'When we reached the Berghof there was nothing to see. Everything was in mist and cloud and it felt very cold though it was not yet winter. They parked and pointed to those very wide steps that went up the cliff to the terrace and said, "Up there, Fräulein." They were not ordinary steps – you must remember them – but huge, wide steps, ten metres wide, and I couldn't see where they went because they followed the curve of the rock out of sight, into the mist. Everyone used to see them sometimes on newsreel film at the cinema when the Führer was receiving important international guests. The Führer was always higher than his guests, do you remember?'

He nodded. She had not talked like this since the first days of her marriage, perhaps not even then. It felt self-indulgent, inconsiderate of her guest. But he had sought her out, had come here, had asked. So she would give it to him, and more if he wanted – which he probably wouldn't. Anyway, he could stop her if he wished. They were both too old to be bothered to take offence.

'Also, the steps were so steep and so awkwardly placed that anyone who ascended them was breathless when he reached the top, and so at a disadvantage to his host. I was, especially as I was carrying my own luggage. But there was no one to greet me, no one at all. I stood at the top, recovering my breath, looking and listening. There was the terrace to the side and the huge window and the great house, but no one to see and nothing to hear except the pounding of my own heart. What I did see was the view. The cloud ended at the last few steps and I stood above it, a great white sea that covered the world below. Only mountain peaks rose above it, like islands. The biggest was the Unterberg peak. They had snow on them and there was also snow nearby, to the sides of the house and above it. That huge window of the great hall, which was used as a living room, remember, was the biggest window I had ever seen. It shone faintly in the light reflected from the snow and cloud. It was all so still, silent and solitary.

'I should have enjoyed it more if I had known I could have remained in solitude for a while and explore in peace. But I felt I had to find someone and explain myself. I was terrified that I might run into the Führer himself and that it would all prove a terrible misunderstanding, that Eva would not be there or would disown me and then I would be there with no excuse in the Führer's private house. I wished that it would prove a ghost house. At that moment I should have preferred any number of ghosts to real people.

'After I got my breath back I picked up my suitcase again and walked in through the door beside this famous window. I intended to call out but I don't think I did. I had no voice. I stood in this huge room facing a huge clock embellished with the bronze eagle. There was also a huge china closet and a huge fireplace and wide chairs and a great long table and two huge paintings of naked women. Just inside, to the left, were some hooks on the wall with a man's hat and coat on one of them. Hitler's, I discovered later. And still nobody there. I felt like bursting into tears, or just running away.

'Then a man came through the door at the far end. He was quite short and he wore black trousers, a white shirt, black tie and a double-breasted field-grey army jacket. It was a plain jacket with no gold braid such as senior Party or military officers wore. There were only silver buttons and a golden Party badge on the left, a swastika armband and the Iron Cross with the black decoration for the wounded. When he saw me he smiled, quite gently, and asked, "What is it, child? Are you lost? Are you looking for someone?"'

Edith sipped her tea. She was unexpectedly enjoying herself, but for her awareness of the unappealing movements her scrawny throat made when she swallowed. Not that she sought to appeal to Hans – the time for that had long passed – but since glimpsing herself in a mirror in the act of swallowing at a dinner party some years ago, she had been conscious of the extravagant oesophageal movements the act now seemed to entail.

'You remember in the Bible,' she continued, 'when the risen Jesus is talking to Mary in the garden and she doesn't recognize him until he says her name? He says, "Mary", and she immediately knows who it is. It was like that for me with the Führer. An unlikely comparison, I know, and quite incredible that I should not immediately have recognized the most famous face in Germany, in Europe, in the world. As you know, he was not one of those famous people who look different in films and photographs to how they are when you meet them. What we see in films is what he was like. Except that his intimate manner, his manner in everyday conversation, was quite different from his appearance in public, when he was making speeches and declaiming. That soft voice, that concentration on you and that formal gallantry that, no matter how artificial you believe it to be, compels a like response. Yet it was precisely this, the – to me – unknown side of him, that made me recognize him. It is strange. I have never understood that.'

'That word in the garden – "Mary" – that single word, whenever I read it, has the power to make me weep,' said Hans.

'And how often do you read the Bible, Hans?'

'About once every twenty-seven years.'

'Of course, I was terribly embarrassed when I realized and didn't know what to say. Actually, I think I started to say "Fräulein Braun" when at that moment Eva swept in and saved me. That too was strange, because she wasn't a woman who normally swept into rooms, or out of them. She was more discreet, though not self-effacing. She wanted to please – men generally, the Führer always – and she did so by sensing what people wanted and becoming it, by not challenging them or asserting herself but being very obliging, above all by being attentive. Attentiveness is the most seductive quality, don't you think? It is so flattering.'

'For me she was not attractive,' he said. 'Well, she was pretty, yes, and she dressed very well, she looked after herself, but she never attracted me. She was stupid. I am always attracted to intelligent women.'

Edith said nothing for a moment, to see if his last remark would prompt in him any self-examination, but it did not. 'If Eva was stupid it was only in the ways that matter least, school ways,' she continued. 'She was shrewd and determined. She knew when to speak and when not to speak. The latter especially. She was the only woman who secured and maintained Hitler's affections, apart perhaps from Geli, his niece who killed herself. And Eva had competition over the years, but she always saw it off. She must have been jealous but she never showed it and it worked, not showing it. Being pleasing worked. But of course she wasn't pleasing only to him.'

'Of course not.'

She was about to continue but he surprised her. 'May we walk in your garden before it is dark?'

FOUR

It almost was dark by the time Wellington boots were found for him. They were not William's old boots – long gone – but those that Michael used when he came over. She took him out through the scullery on to the back lawn. The rain had stopped and the dark racing clouds were broken by streaks of translucent grey-blue spreading across the western horizon. There was a constant buffeting breeze and the lawn – overdue for cutting – was sodden. The cattle beyond the ha-ha raised their heads at the two slow-moving humans, and returned to their grass.

Hans looked back at the house. 'It is a strange shape. Was it built like this?'

'This is only one third of the original. We had to demolish the rest some years after the war. There was a ballroom, many bedrooms and a huge kitchen but it had dry rot and we couldn't afford to repair it. We couldn't afford to staff it, to keep it clean even, let alone that. The rot was apparently let in or made worse by a V-1 pilotless plane, one of the first wonder-weapons. You remember him going on about those?'

'He pinned his hopes upon them.'

'It landed nearby, where that copse is, and the blast is said to have lifted the roof, letting the damp in.'

'Was anyone killed?'

'No.'

'That was fortunate.'

'They were nearly all fortunate here, fortunate to be here.'

'So were we, compared with what happened to many.'

It was not uncongenial to walk with him. He did not demand attention but took an interest in what was around him – not only the house but the park, the dilapidated stables, the old pigeon loft, the copper beech. It was properly dark when they returned, the breeze had dropped and the rain was falling again, heavy penetrating drops. Despite this, he slowly took off Michael's Wellington boots outside in the light from the scullery door. His breathing was laboured.

'You are getting soaked,' she said. 'Come inside.'

'I've nearly finished. Everything takes longer now. The wind makes my asthma worse. Or my angina. I never remember which. They both make me breathless.'

'I'll put your jacket on the Aga. It's quite wet.' Mention of the Aga reminded her of dinner. She realized she was assuming now that he would stay, but she hadn't mentioned it.

He smiled as he took off his jacket. '*Quite* wet. You have become more English than the English, Edith.'

'I sometimes think I am better at it than they are themselves. I see it, they don't.'

He balanced himself with his hand against the scullery wall as he resumed his shoes. 'This must be the first time we have had a walk together, Edith.'

It was not, but she did not say so. They had once walked together at the Berghof when he was briefly there as part of the Führer guard. That was when they had met again, for the first time since school. He had made a great fuss of her, as if they had been closer friends than they actually had. It pleased her because she felt lonely and out of place, unsure of herself and her duties, and any link with home was precious. He paid her attention, when opportunity permitted, and that had meant something; more perhaps than it should have. The day after recognizing each other they had gone for a walk up the footpath to the tea-house. Later they had walked in Berlin, in the Chancellery garden when the shelling was light.

But the walks she remembered best were not those with Hans. They were the glorious alpine walks at the Berghof, heady and exhilarating whether in mist or snow or the dazzling sun. Those walks were with Eva and her sister, Gretl, usually after Eva had persuaded the Führer to stroll with their guests – there were always guests at the Berghof – the short distance up to the tea-house for afternoon tea. There, after holding forth for a while, he invariably fell asleep.

Unlike the walks with Eva, those strolls with Hitler seemed slow and interminable. He was a reluctant walker and agreed only, Edith used to think, because it was a way of humouring Eva without having to sacrifice anything. His nocturnal habits meant that the late afternoons were a dead time for him; he rose late, lunched, then dealt with the routine business that secretaries and adjutants were always bringing him. The main business of the day – his sessions with the generals or senior party people – began in the early evening and would often continue for several hours. The guests would have to make pre-dinner conversation, or if they were lucky watch a film in the private cinema, until Hitler was ready. By the time dinner ended it would be the early hours and by the time he had expounded his views during after-dinner conversation, and permitted Eva to persuade him to bed, the guests looked like corpses in their armchairs and sofas. These were placed so far apart in the great hall that, even when you were not exhausted, sustaining a conversation was like trying to throw a ball to each other.

It was worse for the wives, always on display, always competing. Frau Bormann, who seemed permanently pregnant – despite Bormann having moved his mistress into the marital home – was usually grey with tiredness, barely capable of speech. It was typical of Hitler, Edith later thought, to assume that the world waited for him, never to consider others. But that was the kind of thought you could have only when you were not with him; his presence somehow suppressed all difference, all question, all independent thought, all natural feeling.

And the teas were almost as bad as the late nights. First there were all the preparations – should he wear his hat, or his dark glasses, would it rain, was it too hot or cold, what of the work he had to do? None of this meant anything, Edith later realized; it was merely a way of drawing attention to himself and showing that the great man could be domestic and ordinary. He probably also thought that a walk after lunch to an alpine tea-house with incomparable views was the sort of thing that wealthy, socially superior people generally did. Nearly all the leading Party men thought like that because most of them came from humble or unpretentious backgrounds, the Führer more than anyone. It was strange how much they all wanted to be like those they had pushed aside.

And so they would all embark on the stroll, a straggling party creeping up the winding woodchip path built, maintained and kept permanently clear of snow by – well, by whom? She had never thought until now. By Bormann, ultimately, because he organized everything, but more immediately, by the SS staff, or the guards, or more likely by working parties of prisoners or slave-labourers. The dogs would accompany them – Hitler's German shepherd, Blondi, and Eva's terriers, Negus and Stasi. Mobile mops Hitler used to call the terriers. They at least enjoyed their walk.

In the tea-house they would all be served tea and cakes. The Führer relished cake, but Eva, ever watchful of her trim figure, would merely nibble to keep him company. Then, with everyone in more armchairs, there would be more conversation while the Führer fell asleep. In fact, there was no conversation as normally understood because that was impossible with the Führer. His understanding of conversation was that he would hold forth on a subject – architecture, history, art, the role of women – and it was for his audience to agree and learn. There was never discussion of Party matters or military matters, or politics, the serious things. Those were subjects for orders, not discussion, and anyway were for men only.

Then he would fall asleep – one reason, no doubt, that he couldn't sleep at night – and Eva, sitting next to him, would try valiantly to maintain a general conversation in little more than whispers. This was less like throwing a ball to each other than patting a balloon. It was enervating for everyone and, as she came to know her, Edith used to feel for Eva during such interludes. She kept going, eyes wide open, an encouraging smile for anyone who patted the balloon back up in the air. True, she was playing the part she wanted, mistress of the house, consort of the Führer, the part she had fought hard to attain and never ceased having to defend. True, too, she closed her eyes to almost everything else; the evil she lived with and the suffering beyond her door she simply ignored. But she kept her part up, she kept going to the end. It was a wrong and selfish act, but a superb one; she became the act and it became her. To get what she wanted she had to give constantly of herself, thus doing to an extreme degree, with unfailing courage and in a bad cause, what many women naturally did invisibly throughout their lives. How would it have been if she had had a child? Edith had sometimes wondered. But that, like all other questions, occurred only much later.

The Führer was not the only one who slept at tea. The other somnambulist was Dr Morel, his fat and incompetent personal physician who filled him with pills enough to kill a horse. When he slept his eyes somehow closed from the bottom upwards, making him even more repulsive in sleep than awake. 'If the British have a secret agent in the Führer's circle,' Eva used to say, 'it must be Morel. He is poisoning him with his pills.' He snored, too. But Morel was protected by Bormann.

When Hitler awoke he would resume conversation as if unaware that he had slept. Morel, on the other hand, clearly had no idea where he was for a few seconds; he would sit blinking and looking about him as if he didn't recognize anyone or understand anything.

Then there was the slow walk back to the house, unless Eva decided not to return but to go for her own walk with the dogs. Of course, that had to be negotiated with the Führer first – would the weather change, where would she go, she must be careful, she mustn't be late and so on. It seemed to give him pleasure to show or affect concern about such things, whereas if he had really worried about her going he would simply have forbidden it. And if Edith was lucky, Eva would suggest she accompany her.

Often her younger sister came, too. Gretl, plump, homely, chatty, unsure of herself, always pleased to be included, was dominated by Eva. They would set off at a brisk pace – Eva was a natural sportswoman and always kept herself fit – with the dogs racing ahead through the firs. It was less tiring to walk briskly than to creep along at Hitler's pace and there was a very obvious but never to be mentioned lightening of spirits. Although his presence could never quite suppress the mountain scenery, the white peaks and blue lakes, the varied greens of grasses and trees were suddenly more vivid in his absence. They would talk about everything and nothing – Edith could not now recall a single subject but at the time everything had seemed exciting – and Gretl would be out of breath before either of the others. If Edith wanted to recall Eva at her best, then it was those mountain walks that she remembered.

She thought again now of that day when Eva had welcomed her as she stood, speechless and terrified, before the Führer in the great hall. Eva wore a bright green blouse, white skirt and white shoes. She was fresh, pretty and smiling. She changed her clothes four or five times a day, Edith was to discover.

'She is searching for me,' Eva said to the Führer, 'and I have shamefully not realized she was here.' She held out her hand. 'You poor thing, coming all this way with no one to greet you. You must be hungry and exhausted. Leave your suitcase and come with me. This is no way to begin your new life.'

And so Edith had the job, without ever being asked if she wanted it and without really knowing what it was.

FIVE

'Perhaps you're right, perhaps it was our first walk,' she said as she put Hans's jacket on the Aga. She did not want to remind him of the earlier walks. He might think she shared his fondness for recollection.

'Neither of us could have imagined such a walk in such a place when we were trying to get out of Berlin,' he said. 'At that time we could not even imagine whether we would still be alive an hour after, let alone all these years later.'

'An hour after what, Hans?' she was tempted to ask. Instead, she said, 'I take it you are staying for dinner?'

He raised his bushy eyebrows and creased his forehead. Seeing it again, she remembered it as characteristic, though his eyebrows were not then as bushy. It was like glimpsing a family resemblance in a sibling. 'If that is an invitation, Edith, I am very happy to accept.'

'It will be very plain. Shepherd's pie, made by Mrs Hoath. I shall put it in the oven to warm.'

'I am sure it will be excellent. I have never eaten shepherd's pie.'

She felt a twinge of guilt at not making more of a show of hospitality. 'Hans, there is shepherd's pie and there is Mrs Hoath's shepherd's pie. You are starting at the top.'

They returned to the sitting room, where he had a whisky and she a dry sherry. He made up the fire while she poured.

'I should have brought you a present, a bottle of something at least,' he said.

'You weren't to know you'd have dinner.'

'That is irrelevant, or should be.'

She drew the curtains, listening for the rain but hearing nothing. She loved the many sounds of rain, rain on windows, on roofs, on leaves. Hearing it without feeling it made her feel warm and secure. In the bombed factory where she had met William she had been locked – locked at first, later simply housed – in a shed with a corrugated iron roof. It was cold at night despite the summer days but she had a real bed with blankets and – to her joy – sheets. And it was hers, hers alone. For the first time for months she had a room to herself, even if it was her prison with boarded windows, a cracked uneven concrete floor and locks on the door. Some nights the rain drummed hard on the roof but, also for the first time for months, she felt safe. There were other things to worry about, of course, but feeling safe was an over-whelming relief. It made the other things more bearable.

She and Hans positioned themselves with their drinks as before, she on the sofa adjacent to the fire, he in an armchair facing it. 'Nevertheless, I should have brought something,' he continued. 'I regret not having done so. If regret makes any sense. Do you think it does, ever?'

'I suppose if I felt aggrieved that you hadn't brought any-thing – which I don't – and was then mollified by your expression of regret – for which there is no need – then per-haps it would be a useful kindness to express it, whether or not it was meant. So to that extent it makes sense.'

'But what are you doing when you regret something? You are expressing sorrow for what you did. But can you, really, regret something you did wholeheartedly, believing at the time that it was right? Or even something you did half-heartedly, sensing it was wrong? You might regret that it did not work, or that there were consequences you did not fore-see, or simply that you were found out, but that is not real regret. Real regret, which surely should involve repentance, is a judgement by the present you on the past you. But that past you – the you that did the thing – would have done it again under the same circumstances. The present you is able to regret because now you see more, or see differently. Thus the present you is modified, is different, and therefore no regret you express can be complete because the you that regrets is no longer the you that acted. Or, rather, it is the you that acted plus the you that now perceives.'

He drank more whisky and tilted his head back to look at the ceiling. He appeared to be enjoying himself. Was this why he had sought her out after all these years, to indulge his own pleasure in haranguing and lecturing? Had he done it with all the others he had tracked down? If only with her, was it to be the prelude to full confession and apology; or merely a self-justifying elaboration?

He looked back at her. 'Consider that man we all called the Führer, and never anything else. If he had survived or returned from the dead, and said, "I, Adolf Hitler, deeply and sincerely regret all I did, all the suffering I caused," would we believe him? No. Partly because we would say that he had persuaded himself that regret was the appropriate attitude, just as he hitherto persuaded himself that aggrandizement by conquest and genocide were appropriate actions. He had an infinite capacity for self-delusion, we should say, for believing what he said when he said it, its truth appearing self-evident to him because it was he who was saying it.

'But that is not the only reason we would not believe him. We would also feel that, no matter how sincere he was, no single human being could atone for having wilfully caused such vast suffering. The statement, "It was all my fault and I'm sorry", would be ludicrously, laughably inadequate. The very concept of regret breaks down when we try to apply it to someone who wrought such deliberate and massive wrong. The Christian doctrine of atonement – confession, penance, restitution, absolution – might work for you and me, but for him? What penance could he do, what restitution could he possibly make? Who – in God's name – could grant Hitler absolution? Only God Himself, the believer might say. But you have to be a real believer to accept the God who would do that.

'No. The Hitler who regrets could not be the Hitler who did what he did. Such an evil-doer, on such a scale, could not possibly feel genuine regret unless he had changed so fundamentally that he really was no longer the same person. His heart had not the capacity for regret. Adolf Hitler could not regret what Adolf Hitler did. If he could, he would not be Adolf Hitler.'

His words lapped around her like lukewarm water, neither hot enough to provoke nor cold enough to avoid. It was all pointless so far as she was concerned. Nevertheless, half-formed quibbles, points she could pick up if she chose, floated in and out of her mind. Did Hitler regret the suicide of Geli, the step-niece who lived with him and who surely shared his bed, or whatever he used for his practices, and who shot herself in his Munich flat with his own pistol for the love and lack of him? His last words to the weeping girl were shouted: 'For the last time, no!' He saw to it that there was no inquest. But he kept her room exactly as she had left it, locked, with not even Eva, her successor, allowed in. And ever afterwards her portrait hung in the Berghof. Of course he would say he regretted her death, but would he regret what had made her wretched enough to kill herself, his simultaneous use and denial of her? The only test of such regret would be if he changed. But change for the Führer – even for the then would-be Führer – was impossible, he would have argued. To be Führer was to be most strongly and inflexibly yourself.

Geli's successor – young like herself – was also often wretchedly neglected. She too once shot herself, for love of and lack of him, but not seriously. It was put about that it was an accident while cleaning the pistol. Just the sort of thing a young girl like Eva did at home alone in the evenings. It would not have looked good for an aspiring Führer to leave in his wake a litter of female suicides.

But Edith said none of this to Hans, content to leave him to the generalities he clearly enjoyed. Generalities were one thing, individual actions, actual betrayals, what you did at that very moment, in that very place – were quite another. If speaking in these general terms helped him come to terms with his own betrayal, so much the better. If, on the other hand, it was his way of not approaching it, of continuing to hide from it, then so much the worse for him. If he really wanted to bring it to the surface but was unable to do so himself, she could do it for him in a sentence.

'I must go and look at the dinner.' She got up slowly because armchairs had become so low of late and her knees so painful. 'Pour yourself more whisky.'

She still hadn't made up her mind where they should eat. At the kitchen table would be easiest and most suited to the meal. On trays before the fire in the sitting room would be cosiest. The dining room with the long candlelit table that Mrs Hoath polished so religiously, so rarely used, would convey a sense of occasion; but the room would be cold with disuse and she was not sure she wanted to dignify the occasion in this way. It would feel too much like a concession, though precisely what she would be conceding, she couldn't say. After all, he was perfectly friendly and respectable and she was beginning to like him, in a not very serious way, for his sincere if laboured and ultimately futile quest for understanding. If that was what it was.

However, the dining room would mean that she could show off a little without being too obvious. William's family silver was almost never used these days, nor the Royal Doulton plate, and the table was a fine Georgian piece. She would ask him which he preferred; he would doubtless say it was up to her.

'The dining room, of course,' he said immediately, holding up his hands. 'We must make as grand an occasion of this as we can, even if there is no one to witness our grandeur. I brought an English dinner jacket in case this was what you wanted, but I wasn't going to mention it. Now I can. I will change and you can change into your most beautiful dress.'

'I'm afraid I no longer possess beautiful dresses. There is no beauty left to adorn.'

'Nonsense, Edith, you are as beautiful as ever. And shall I explain why this is not mere flattery? Shall I tell you why it is true?'

She smiled.

'It is because you are still Edith.' He held up his hand. 'Do not protest that this is inevitable, that you have no choice. You do. By the choices you make throughout your life, some big ones that you knew would change it – shall I marry him? Shall I have a child? Shall I live in England? – and by countless small daily choices that make up the texture of life you have become what you are, and you have become most fully yourself, Edith. I can see it and sense it. Everyone has such choices but many choose in such ways, big and small, that they never fulfil their potential, never become most fully themselves. It is through fear, usually, fear of exposure, fear of failure, fear of others, fear of loneliness, fear of fear. Fear drives out not only love but all else, save itself.' He paused, and contemplated his brown shoes. 'You see, that water-under-the-bridge metaphor for the past is wrong because we are not on the bridge. We are in the water. We are in there with it. That is why the past matters.'

'You should have been a pastor, Hans.'

He smiled and rubbed his right cheek with his hand. 'I used to think I might, when I was in the labour camp. If ever I got out, I thought, I shall become a pastor, live simply, plainly, gratefully, thank God and devote my life to others. I associated it with solitude, and in the camp where you are never, ever alone that appealed strongly. After my release, back in Germany, the first time I walked into a room and shut the door and was alone in the room, I burst into tears. I had not wept for years but it was so beautiful to be alone. Yes, I was tempted to become a pastor.'

'Do you believe in God?'

'That was one problem. There were others, perhaps more serious. Busyness, necessity, work, domesticity, relations with others – all these things are spurs to achievement but enemies to dedication. They intervene. The world is a con-spiracy against sustained endeavour. And so I did not become a pastor and the world was spared my sermons.'

For the first time in many years she wished she had a cig-arette. It was becoming the kind of conversation she associated with youth, self-indulgence, leisure, playing with big fat themes that seemed too excitingly important until fed into the mincer of daily life. In those days one always had a cigarette. 'Some people would say that all these choices you mentioned, these components of our lives, are not really choices at all but illusions. It feels as if we are choosing this husband or that way of life but in fact our material circumstances or our personalities determine that we inevitably make the choices we do. We make them because we are what we are. Character is action.'

Irritatingly, he was shaking his head before she finished. 'All arguments for determinism or attributions to fate are manifestations of fear, ways of escaping individual responsibility. And if they were true, regret would make no sense at all, since everything would be unavoidable. Yet I think you want to believe it possible for individuals to regret particular things. Am I right, Edith?'

She fixed her eyes on his lips. Perhaps he was coming to it now. 'If you don't want to look them in the eye, look at their lips,' William had told her, when they used to laugh about how they met. 'It appears to your interrogator that you are looking him in the eye but it's nothing like as much strain.' Hans used to have a sensitive mouth, she remembered, with full lips, but they were thinner and less expressive now. In those days his sensitive mouth undermined the impression of impersonal military efficiency he sought to convey. He was plainly unsure of himself then, at least less sure than he liked to appear, and that had made him more attractive.

'Consider Magda Goebbels,' he continued. 'Was what she did determined for her or was it her choice? And if she joined us now would it make as little sense for her to express regret as it would the Führer, or would it make more?'

The image of Magda Goebbels, tall, eloquent, confident, sweeping into the great hall at the Berghof, glass in hand, taking the sofa for herself, crossing her long legs with a rustle of dress and silk stocking, directing the full beam of her attention upon the man – or, if there was more than one, the senior man – was immediately discomforting. Even now Edith felt almost physically displaced by this formidable image, and ignored by Magda as she had been in life. It was not that Magda was actively unfriendly to other women; she simply had no time for most of them. She was exactly what so many women feared and admired: attractive, intelligent, reputedly intellectual, with a glamorous past and, with six children, triumphantly fecund. Stories of her husband's frequent and flagrant infidelities did nothing to diminish her; indeed, her reputation seemed to gain by them.

'She would regret what she did,' said Edith eventually. 'She could not fail to regret. If there is a hell she will spend eternity pierced by regret and unable to express it or undo it. No woman – no mother – could do what she did and not regret. It is one thing for Hitler to murder six million Jews he didn't know and not regret, but quite another to believe that she who murdered her own six little ones could rest in peace.'

'But if she were mad?'

'Magda was not mad.'

'Mad for the Führer? Madly in love with him?'

'Perhaps. But she was not mad.'

'I have studied her life. There is a consistency of obsession throughout. In her youth she was madly in love with the Zionist Arlosorff, she started learning Hebrew, she nearly married him, his sister became her best friend. Then she falls madly in love with Günther Quandt, the industrialist, the man of power, and marries him. Then she goes once – once only – to hear the young National Socialist Josef Goebbels speak. She immediately falls madly for him too and so becomes a Nazi, no longer a Zionist. So she marries him instead. Then she has intense affairs with Hanke and Naumann, successive permanent secretaries at the propaganda ministry. And all the time she is fanatical about the Führer, her children always take him birthday presents, they sing for him, she entertains him, and in the end she kills herself and murders them because of him, because he is dead.

'Those striking eyes of hers, those hungry staring eyes – you must remember them, Edith – and that obsessive energy, that passion for powerful men and causes. Was one a symptom of the other? First Zionism, then Nazism, of all things. If it hadn't been Nazism and Hitler, then who? Marxism and Stalin? Any powerful man with a powerful ism. If she had been born to an earlier age it would have been Protestantism and Luther. Whatever the cause of this passion for passion – an imbalance, perhaps, an inner vacuum, a void she had to fill – it merits the term madness. Psychiatrists do not like that word, I know, because it is not specific, it means anything and nothing, it is a way of not describing something. But it means one big thing that psychiatrists are too learned to notice: it means the inability to connect with ordinary, everyday life, all the commonplace emotions and common perceptions, everything true and unremarkable. Only someone incapable of that could possibly believe that the world would end with Hitler. Granted, it was understandable to fear for her children in Russian hands, and perhaps understandable – if not reasonable – to fear for them in a world without Nazism. But virtually every other mother on this planet would have accepted the offer to get her children out. Especially if they were offered, as Magda was, a real chance to escape with them. Kempka offered it, Speer offered it, even the Führer himself, he offered it.'

And that kitchen drudge, thought Edith, recalling the pale girl who worked in the Reich Chancellery kitchens. Right at the end she had approached Magda, soft spoken, stammering, nervous. A girl who had nothing, no home to go to, no future, no looks, no personality that anyone noticed, yet she had screwed up her courage to approach the imperious Magda and stammer, 'If you please, honourable lady, if you please, your children, I will take them, I will take them out.' She, Magda and Edith had coincided in a corridor in the upper bunker, where the bombs and shells were louder and shook the walls and floors. The lighting flickered, the hum and smell of generators was worse, the atmosphere stuffier.

Magda hesitated for less than a second, her face rigid and her lips compressed. Then she swept on without replying, as if it were impossible for her to engage in discussion with someone so lowly, or even to acknowledge that such a person had spoken. To be charitable – it was not easy for Edith to be charitable about Magda – she might have been too upset to speak. The girl's final faltering, 'Please, honourable lady,' was delivered to her imperious back. The girl was almost in tears and Edith struggled to control her own. They gazed at each other in unspoken recognition, their backs against the cold dirty grey walls of the corridor. The girl's thin face was riven with despair, her protruding lower lip trembled, her protruding eyes were wet and piteous. They were not her children, they were nothing to do with her, she might never have spoken to them, only heard their laughter or seen them shepherded, crocodile fashion, along the corridor. Helpless herself, she had offered herself. Edith could not recall how they parted and never saw her again. Who knew what became of her? The thought of her still made her want to weep.

She poured herself more sherry. 'Magda was not mad.'

'Did you see her afterwards?'

'Alive or dead?'

'Both.'

Again, his questions recalled her early interrogations. 'What happened to Goebbels?' William had asked.

'He killed himself, along with his wife.'

'How?'

'He shot himself. Probably her too, unless she took poison. Or maybe they got the guards to shoot them both. However they did it, they are dead.'

'Did you see their bodies?'

'Yes, in the garden, not far from Hitler's and Eva's. I could see them from the top of the bunker steps. They were on fire.'

'They were recognizable?'

'Yes, they had not burned very much.'

'What time was this?'

'After Hitler and Eva had killed themselves, late afternoon or early evening.'

'Didn't they have children?'

'Six, five girls and a boy, aged five to thirteen.'

'What happened to them?'

'Their mother poisoned them, I told you. With Stumpfegger, the doctor.'

'How?'

'They were given potassium cyanide, the capsules we all had, in their bedtime drinks. They were told it would help them sleep. But Helga, the eldest, realized something was happening and I think they had to force her.'

'Did you know the children?'

'Of course. I used to play with them, to help entertain them. Before they went to bed every night we sang with them, Traudl Junge and the other secretaries and I. We were part-singing together when the bombing and shelling was worse on the day Hitler and Eva died, I told you. It was good to sing, they enjoyed it. We knew there were— there were— plans for them, but we didn't realize it would be so soon. We didn't want to think about it. They were all in their white nightgowns.'

She remembered how coolly she had related this to her interrogator. Is youth really so callous? she later asked herself. Perhaps; according to the dictates of nature it has above all to ensure its own survival until it has replicated itself and ensured the next generation. Then, when you are no longer necessary and no longer matter, you can afford to feel on behalf of others. Then you get ill and die.

But her control did not last the interrogation. William broke it for her, unintentionally. She remembered clearly, even now, how he put down his pen and sat back in his chair, looking at her. The sun on his shoulders made her think how hot he must be in his battledress tunic and thick hairy shirt. The sun prevented her from seeing his face clearly but she heard him murmur in English, as to himself, 'All my pretty ones? Did you say all? Oh hellcat. Did you say all?'

She must have looked questioningly because he sat forward again, hands clasped, elbows on the desk. 'Shakespeare,' he said quietly, 'from *Macbeth*. Macduff has just been told of the murder of his wife and all his children.' His expression, which she could see now, was thoughtful. 'All his pretty ones, all his pretty chickens, he calls them. All.'

It was the repetition of 'all' that did it. How, or why, she did not know. With no notice, no premonition, she was overwhelmed by tears. Her eyes filled, she couldn't speak, a great sob broke from her and she sat before him shaking and weeping. She had no idea for how long. Yet through it all she was aware that he was not embarrassed, that he let her go on without trying to stop her. Eventually he stood and took from his pocket a very large khaki handkerchief – it could only have been an army handkerchief – which he handed to her across the desk before sitting again, hands clasped as before. Even while her tears continued she remained clearly aware of him, of his expression, his tone and his words. Later, she often thought that this was the moment it had started for them both. But although he was a man who could provoke and participate in great emotion, he was – disappointingly – not a man to talk about it. His handkerchief had smelled of recent washing. She was grateful and, even as she dried her eyes, wondered where she could get one for herself. When she started to apologize he stopped her.

'You must acknowledge it in order to cope with it,' he said slowly, choosing his German as if crossing a stream on slippery stepping stones. 'When Macduff is urged to take comfort in revenge, to dispute it like a man, he says, "I shall do so; but I must also feel it as a man." You were put through the wringer in those last days but you had no time to feel it then. Now that you do, you should. It will always be with you but you must accept it, let it become part of your skin, your texture, then it won't harm you.'

For years she thought she had successfully done that but now, faced with Hans, she was less sure. It would be absurd and humiliating to break down before him as she had before William, but that was how she felt when talking about it. In fact, it was remembering and imagining that made her feel it; talking might, paradoxically, be a way of not feeling it.

'Yes,' she said, after sipping her sherry. 'I did see her alive and dead. I saw her immediately afterwards, when she came downstairs from the children's rooms – they were on the upper floor, if you remember. She looked appalling – drained, distracted, shocked, as if she had been disembowelled but was still alive. She walked past me without even seeing me, I think. Well, no great change there, perhaps. She would do that with Eva herself sometimes. Later I saw her again. She was crying. But then I saw her sitting at the big table with Stumpfegger, who had helped her do it. They were playing solitaire or something,

something commonplace and ridiculous. The last I saw of her alive was on her husband's arm, climbing the steps up to the garden as if they were getting married. She was very elegantly dressed – she and Eva were alike in that way – and she was wearing on her breast the little gold Party insignia that the Führer had given her. Did you see him do that, when he was saying goodbye to people that morning?'

'I never saw the Führer that day. I was in and out of the bunker, taking messages to the High Command.'

'Well, you know, he shuffled around, shaking hands with people. He shook hands with me. His hand was very limp, passive, like a cold dead fish in one's own, but I was happy to get no closer because his breath smelled so. It was truly horrible, probably all that vegetarian food and those thousands of pills that that medical idiot Morel filled him with. His face was as white as chalk and he said little or nothing to most people. But when he came to Magda he held her hand for a long time and his cheek twitched, but he still didn't say anything. Then suddenly he took his own Party insignia off his grey jacket and pinned it to her lapel. It took a long time because his fingers shook. She burst into tears. No one had seen Magda cry before. I wouldn't have thought she could. Anyway, she died wearing that badge. I think she and Goebbels walked up to the garden themselves in case nobody would carry their bodies out. With Hitler dead, discipline was weakening, everything was becoming looser. People smoked, as I told you.'

'Yet not mad, you say? Only mad about the Führer. And capable of regret?'

'If there is a hell, then baffled regret is all it has to be for her. There is no need for torturing flames. Mere consciousness would do. I hope there is and I hope she's in it.'

'And what of Fegelein, Edith? Should anyone regret Fegelein, do you think?'

'I must look at the dinner,' she said. 'And then we must change.'

SIX

She had three long dresses, all old and unfashionable and none worn during the past three years at least. More likely five, she reflected, recalling her reluctant attendance at the last hunt ball. Her last, anyway; a dreadful, loud, raucous affair of thumping pop music and drunken young people.

In charitable moments she was prepared to acknowledge that perhaps the young had always been like that. She remembered drunken parties in Berlin at the end, with Armageddon approaching and no future that anyone could imagine. One party in particular had been an affair of almost Roman licence as the almost Roman discipline of the defending garrison collapsed, provoking a sexual abandon that the hunt ball never, thankfully, approached. But even that desperate abandon had been more stylish than the loutish staggerings and gropings of the hunt ball.

ALAN JUDD

There were uniforms at both, of course, but the Nazis – albeit one shouldn't think anything good about the Nazis – were world class when it came to uniforms. And with cars, all those beautiful black Mercedes. But people could dance then, perhaps that was the difference; they danced to music, not only at the same time as the music, and it was music with melody as well as rhythm. You varied your dance with the music and, above all, you danced with someone. She did not understand the modern enthusiasm for monkey-scratch dancing, as she privately called it, which you might as well do by yourself. In fact, they did do it by themselves, since the loud music was so isolating.

It was better in every way to dance with someone, even if all you had to dance to was the single record that Eva had found with the phonograph, and which she played over and over again. 'Blood-red roses tell you of happiness,' was the refrain. Well, blood ran red in the streets of Berlin that night, Hitler's last birthday, ten days before the end. The British and Americans bombed the city for twenty-four hours con- tinuously, a birthday present from the Allies. Perhaps the carnage in the streets made them all the more keen to dance in what was left of the Führer's Chancellery apartment. There were holes in the walls, the lights came and went, part of the ceiling was down and blasts shook the building. Yet they danced as if it were the last dance in the world. The destruction that was about to engulf them heightened their lascivious abandon.

It was all Eva's doing, her idea, her energy and organization; it was she who rounded up all those Waffen-SS officers, she who found all that champagne, she who kept breaking the dance to put the record on again. Breaking a dance that was in her case Fegelein's embrace. The scene was still vivid to Edith: the tall handsome young officer – and didn't he know it – holding Eva up in his strong arms, their gazing into each other's eyes as he slowly, very slowly, lowered her the length of his body, breast to breast, crotch to crotch, all the while locked into each other's eyes. And all the while Gretl, his wife, Eva's sister, pregnant, lonely and unknowing, waited for news in the Berghof.

The Führer, of course, never danced. He saw no point in it. His pursuit of power was too pure, too aesthetic almost, to countenance such frivolity. He'd have been no good at it. One instinctively knew that; perhaps he did. Would he even have been Führer if he had been a dancer? Did Mussolini dance, did Stalin? She didn't know. Napoleon didn't, someone had told her.

Nor did Hitler attend the party. He remained many floors down in the deep bunker, ashen, brooding, trembling, his sentences breaking up and his words becoming incoherent whenever the bombs fell close. He couldn't have borne it above ground in the ruined Chancellery, which even when it wasn't shaking was shedding dust from its walls and ceilings. But the dancers noticed that only in the uneasy seconds it took for Eva, bending swiftly, to put on the record again. She wore a new dress – yet another new dress, even then – of silver-blue brocade. It had ridden up as far as her stocking tops when Fegelein lowered her the length of his body. She was careless of it, clinging to his uniform shoulders, her eyes locked in his.

The image was so vivid that it took Edith a few moments to recall herself to the present, which was her own familiar but no longer welcome image in the cheval mirror in her bedroom. The wardrobe doors hung open and on her bed lay discarded dresses, but she was still undecided about the one she had on. Long sleeved and high necked, it would at least be warm. It, too, was brocade but black with white lace cuffs and collar. It looked very old fashioned, even to her old-fashioned eyes, almost Victorian. She couldn't remember why she had bought it; presumably because of that. She must have thought it fashionable then, whenever 'then' was. It couldn't have been very long ago, the last ten years perhaps, because if it had she would have remembered. She often forgot things because they hadn't happened long enough ago. She didn't like the dress now but it was comfortable and warm and hid far more than it revealed; and it was already on. She couldn't be bothered to change again and, anyway, it wasn't as if she were on public display. At least she had washed her hair earlier in the day. She didn't need anything around her neck, with that dress, but it did demand earrings.

She took her jewellery box from the drawer and picked through it, yet again wishing her hands weren't so obviously those of an old crone. Thank goodness the rest of the body was hidden. Her jewellery, she had long ago decided, would go to her daughter-in-law. She had already given her some of the finer pieces but they remained, so far as she knew, unworn. Probably too old to be fashionable and not old enough to be valuable. Like people in old age. Most humans died while still in the redundant stage, old enough to be useless but not old enough to become interesting again.

Her fingers hovered above a small sapphire earring mounted in a delicate filigree of gold. It was strikingly blue, appearing to move with the light as though there were eyes captive within it. Her first thought was that she could not possibly wear it, since it had no sibling. That was lost long ago in the tunnel in Berlin. Her second thought was also that she could not possibly wear it because it would be too obvious a gesture, even if, being a man, Hans might not notice its solitary state. And even if he did he would not realize its significance, unless she told him. Yet if not now, when? She had never worn it since that time. Either it remained never, or it was now. She took it from the box and carefully attached it to her right ear.

Hans wore a dinner jacket with a winged collar and a

clumsily knotted bow tie. He must have had the suit in his car and, although everything was slightly crumpled, he still made, even now, a respectable figure of a man. Suits always improved men, she thought, almost as much as uniform. He had poured himself another drink and stood by the sitting-room fire he had made up. He looked a little too pleased with himself, almost proprietorial.

'As I said, Edith, you are still beautiful,' he said, before she had the chance to speak.

'I'll call you when dinner is on the table.'

He laughed. 'No, but you are, not beautiful as in your youth, of course, but differently beautiful. Don't try to palm me off. I mean it.'

She stayed despite herself. 'I was never beautiful, Hans. Attractive maybe, because I was young. Youth itself is attractive. But not beautiful. Eva was beautiful, not I.'

'Eva?' He raised his hands and furrowed his brow in a pantomime gesture. The little photographer's assistant from Munich? 'As I said before, pretty, yes, well dressed I grant you – once she, or the Party, or the German people could afford to pay for it. Flirtatious? Certainly. But beautiful? No. She lacked the inner quality that real womanly beauty always suggests, the inaccessible something that makes you want to go on and on and on, trying to reach it, trying to possess it. Perhaps ultimately a moral quality.'

'So all beautiful women are moral?'

'All beauty is moral. Eva had no beauty and Eva was not moral.'

'I never knew you were such a romantic, Hans.'

'I was, and am. I am romantic about everything, above all about the past.'

'Is that why you are here?'

He smiled with his lips only. 'Perhaps.'

She fetched the dinner, lit candles in the dining room, placing four on the long table and seating herself at one end, Hans at the other. The distance was absurd but appropriate to the formalities of their surroundings and their dress.

'You have no German wine?' he asked after glancing at the French table wine she produced.

'We have, somewhere in William's cellar, but I didn't think to get it up. I am sorry.'

'Never mind. I shall be wine waiter and keep it by me. It would be ridiculous to stand it between us where neither of us could reach it.' He poured hers and returned to his end of the table.

They raised their glasses. Neither spoke.

'What sort of pie did you call this?' he asked.

'Shepherds.'

He chewed his food slowly and thoroughly. When he swallowed his prominent Adam's apple rose and fell with perfect mechanical precision. She wondered again how noticeable her own swallowing was.

'Would you say,' he continued, 'that Eva Braun was a moral woman?'

She shrugged. 'I would say that she was neither more nor less moral than many people. Which is to say, she was neither scrupulously moral nor dramatically immoral. She had a moral sense and was capable of moral discrimination independently of her own desires. There were one or two occasions when for essentially moral reasons she took actions that could have threatened her position. But overall she closed her eyes and shut her ears to what should have awakened her, choosing to suspend her moral sense rather than allow it to prevent her having what she wanted. She was selfish, often shallow, sometimes plain silly. But she accepted the consequences of her decisions – a whole series of decisions, spread over years – with courage, even dignity.'

'You have clearly thought a great deal about her.'

'Hardly at all until this moment. I rarely think of her. Or of anything of that time. Because you ask me, I answer, but I am thinking aloud; I don't know what thoughts are there until I say them.'

'Do you blame her?'

'One has to.'

He raised his eyebrows. 'But reluctantly?'

'With some reservations.'

'Which?'

'Children. She always made great efforts with other people's children, playing with them, remembering their birthdays, taking them on expeditions, spending time with them when their parents wouldn't. Even the children of Martin Bormann, her greatest enemy and rival for the Führer's attention, the man who would have had her killed if he could. They hated each other but they both knew better than to complain to the Führer, since they both understood him better than anyone else did. She used to have to take Bormann's arm when they went into dinner at the Berghof and he would say nasty things to her smilingly, knowing she had to accept it and smile back. And it was his arms that carried her body up the bunker steps, at least part of the way. But you must know that.'

'I wasn't in the bunker when that happened.'

'Didn't any of your other witnesses tell you?'

'My "witnesses"?' He smiled. 'Yes, they did.'

'And you must have found Bormann hateful, too, didn't you? Having to work under him?'

'He was very senior and I was very junior. The distance between our ranks was so great that personal qualities were unable to cross the divide. They were irrelevant.'

'Yet Eva took his children on picnics, took them swimming, helped with them when his wife was busy having more children, as she always was, and when he was busy with his mistress, as he always was. She would have loved to have children of her own, she said, but the Führer would not consider it. It was the same with marriage. He was married to Germany, he said. His work would not permit him to behave towards his wife as a married man should. He used to say: "I wouldn't be a good head of a family. I would consider it irresponsible of me to start a family when I could not devote myself to my wife sufficiently. Besides, I want no children of my own. I find that the offspring of geniuses usually have it hard in this world. One expects of them the importance of their famous predecessor and doesn't forgive them for being average. Besides, they are mostly cretins."'

He looked as if he doubted her. 'He said that?'

'That is how he spoke,' she replied, with emphasis. 'It is what he believed. You knew him. You must have heard him yourself on such subjects.'

'He did not speak like that with soldiers. With secretaries he could be more confiding, I suppose, but not with soldiers.'

'The point is, Eva went out of her way to be kind to children, any children. I think that is something to her credit.'

He sipped his wine and shook his head. 'Darwinian necessity, the natural instinct, the desire and lasting pleasure of most women. It may have beneficial and moral results, it may be good in itself, but essentially she was acting as nature intended in order to ensure the survival of the next generation. Feeling like that about children and behaving towards them in a way that expresses that feeling was not a moral act. She could not help it.'

'She might have cared nothing for them, nothing for anyone beyond herself. She might have been cruel or indifferent.'

'She was indifferent, indifferent to hundreds of thousands of children whose murders were ordered by the man she loved. Indifference is surely the deepest and most lasting cruelty.'

'I don't believe she knew about all that, at least not in any detail. None of us did.'

'She was in a position to know. She simply did not want to. She could have known, she could have listened less selectively. She didn't have to ask lots of questions. She just closed her eyes and her ears, as you said.'

'Didn't we all? Didn't we all allow ourselves to be spellbound, while he lived?'

He looked at her for some seconds before replying. 'As much as we wanted to be.'

She put down her fork. 'So are we all war criminals? There's so much about them in the papers and on television these days. The farther we get from it and the fewer survivors, the more fuss there is. Perhaps all of us who were there should be arrested for not having tried to stop it at the time. Is that what you think?'

He paused again. 'I do not hold with this modern

enthusiasm for retrospective legislation. It is dangerous and unfair.'

'But even if Eva had opened her eyes and unstopped her ears, what could she have done? What was it reasonable to expect her to do? Given that when she first got involved with him he was simply Herr Hitler, the Bavarian politician—'

'Didn't he like to call himself Herr Wolf then?'

'If you say so.'

'And didn't she seduce him?'

Edith had picked up her fork, but now she put it down again. 'She was seventeen. She was working for Hoffmann, Hitler's friend, the Munich photographer. Hitler comes into the shop when she is up a ladder getting something from the shelves. She knows he can see up her skirt, up her legs, up her thighs. She lets him. It probably flatters her to realize she can attract someone as easily as that. She is in no danger, she doesn't know who he is. She is not the first young girl to react like that. Then Hoffmann sends her out to get some sausages and beer and they eat together, although Hitler doesn't eat meat, of course. She tells a funny story about how she knocked a box of film off a top shelf, which fell on to the cat, which ran out of the door as the bakery boy was coming in with bread, causing him to trip so that he fell headlong into a display of camera tripods, which fell on top of him while the bread rolled everywhere. Also, they talked about plays, musicals and American films. Afterwards, when

Hoffmann told her who had been with them, she still didn't know who he was. He was just another older man with a slouch hat and a little moustache and a collar an inch wide of his neck, making him look like a turtle sticking its head out of its shell. She was, though, struck by his eyes. They were so blue and so intense. And she became interested when she realized he was a minor celebrity. She liked celebrities.' Defending Eva was not something Edith was used to doing, even to herself, but Hans had irritated her. It felt uncomfortable but necessary and her discomfort made her more assertive than she might have been. 'I know all this because she told me about it. She used to talk to me, especially when we were alone in the Berghof. She had no one else to confide in, I suppose, not being very close to either of her sisters. Anyway, she was not the first girl to like celebrities. If that is a fault, it's a very common one.'

'So then she seduced him?'

'They went to plays and musicals sometimes and sometimes they ate together. Hoffmann was a keen matchmaker and arranged things at his studio to bring them together. She soon became interested in Herr Hitler, perhaps the more so because her father was against him and said he was a madman and a fanatic. She only ever talked to him about trivial things – musicals and films, things he liked, never politics, so he felt easy with her, he relaxed. She couldn't have gone ahead and seduced him, just like that, even if she had wanted. He would have run away and she was wise enough not to try. Anyway, there were other women in his life, principally Geli, of course, with whom he lived. Or with whom he shared his apartment – these things were never quite clear with Hitler. And other women, powerful, rich, political women. They liked to talk politics with him, to feel part of politics, but Eva sensed he didn't like that. He simply accepted their help. Really, he didn't like women in politics. He wanted them in the kitchen, looking like the Austrian hausfraus he remembered from his childhood. And later there was that mad Englishwoman who was so in love with him, that aristocrat whom he flattered and used for what she could tell him about Mr Churchill and his plans before the war. She, too, tried to kill herself over him. As did Eva, as you know, when he was busy and ignoring her and she felt that people around him were against her. Some of them were. His adjutant then, Bruckner, called her a "quiet, stupid cow". But she was not stupid, just not very educated and lacking intellectual curiosity, like most people. She was clever enough to be quiet, which Hitler appreciated more the busier he became. Once I heard him say – not to me – "She keeps my mind off other things, which is a rest for me sometimes." She dressed for him, she did whatever he wanted in the bedroom, she made a fuss of him, she made it easy for him when he was with her. And the more difficult everything else became, the more he appreciated that. He used to say

that the only beings he could trust absolutely were Eva and
his dog, Blondi. She knew how to get a man and keep him.
It was the clever women who were stupid.'

'Yet she betrayed him.'

SEVEN

Edith listened for the rain. Although it didn't sound on the dining-room windows as on those in the sitting room, it was louder and steadier now, a relentless background drumming. 'Steady rain,' William would have called it. One up from soft rain. He had a word for every variety of rain. 'Gives a good soaking,' he invariably added.

One of the candles was threatening to drip on to the table. She got up and removed it, holding it upside down over the holder until the wax dripped in, then she replaced it. Candlelight suited the wood-panelled room, hiding its many blemishes and making it appear warmer than it felt.

'I know what you are thinking, Edith,' Hans continued. 'You are thinking that "betrayal" is a strong word for me to use.'

When she sat again she wrapped her long dress around her legs, against the draught. 'That thought crossed my mind.'

'But she did, didn't she?'

'It depends upon what you mean by betrayal', would have been the natural response, but he might by extension have applied it to himself and she did not want to let him off that hook so easily. Yet in fairness it could apply to him; what seemed betrayal to the betrayed may be justifiable self-preservation to the betrayer. Or it may have been inescapable, unavoidable, something over which he had no choice. Or it may have been a very powerful reaction which he could have resisted and which he might now regret, but which he was at the time too weak, too tired, too fearful to resist. She herself well knew how paralysing – how literally, physically, paralysing – fear could be. She had stood in that tunnel with the two Russian soldiers, wanting to run, seeing the chance to run, not panicking but calculating and reasoning, reckoning her chances, willing herself to seize the moment, yet unable to move her legs. They were not weak, not trembling, not even locked, just unresponsive to the messages she sent them. There was no question of refusal – everything in her wanted to run – but it was as if they were simply disconnected. Perhaps it had been like that for Hans when he tried to engage his moral function; if he had tried.

'I don't know,' she said, 'whether in fact she did betray him.'

'Others who were there thought she did. We thought so, in the guard force. And it's the fact that counts in betrayal, the act, not the thought.'

'Is it?' Was he preparing to be hard on himself, encouraging her to be hard on him too so that he could feel less guilty? Well, he would have to wait for that. 'It depends which facts you choose.'

'I mean the fact of her affair with Fegelein.'

'Is an affair a fact?'

An accident, a remark, the murder of one's children, could all be facts, but what constituted an affair? A multiplicity of facts, surely, and layers of interpretation, intention, wish, sympathy and mutual imagination. It was not simply the sex, though going to bed with someone was undeniably a fact. But that was an event, not an affair. Even if it were repeated and became a series of events, it might seem an affair to one party while remaining a series of events to the other. An affair, surely, required that both parties see it as such, but even then it might not be seen as such by the rest of the world. It was not, after all, necessary to go to bed in order to have an affair, an affair of the heart, an affair of the mind, an intense emotional and intellectual sympathy which could bring two people closer to each other than to anyone else, but which to the outside world would not constitute an affair.

To call Eva's relations with Fegelein, the young SS cavalry officer, an affair was at once to exaggerate and to simplify. She remembered his arrival at the Berghof. All the girls did because for once this was no hard-bitten middle-aged general with battles to fight and arguments to win, or self-important Party functionary with no time for frippery and gallantry. This was a tall, handsome blond charmer, with the prestigious but not too demanding role of liaison officer between Hitler and Himmler, who was hardly ever there. Fegelein was thus neither buried by work nor always present, so there was no time to tire of him. Decorated from the Russian front, a gifted horseman and dancer, his master's – Himmler's – favourite, with a reputation for bravery and brutality, an aggressive humour and a ready smile, he might have been made for unmarried women, or married. He knew it, that was the trouble. His good opinion of himself was as obvious as his tailored black uniform. You saw and heard it in his undiscriminating confident manner, which by assuming acceptance usually gained it.

He instantly gained it with Eva and poor Gretl, her goose of a sister as Fegelein himself had called her at first. But not with Edith. Her own lack of response had troubled her at the time, she remembered. Seeing all the other females in a state of arousal had made her worry that she lacked something. He was attractive, she did not deny, but he didn't attract her. It wasn't only his self-satisfaction, nor the

101

bullying arrogance he displayed with junior staff, nor his toadying to his superiors. It was, rather, the impression of untrustworthiness, particularly those shallow restless blue eyes that became still only when they settled on someone he wanted to impress. It was an obvious, unremitting questing for advantage. If you talked to him at a social occasion he was constantly looking over your shoulder to see whether there was anyone better. And if you were that person he fixed you with a hungry attention which it was impossible for you to believe you merited, unless you were like him, or unless you were Eva Braun. Privately, Edith had contrasted him with Hans, of all people, honest, trustworthy Hans.

But for poor Eva Fegelein's attentiveness came as water to a parched plant. Hitler had already begun to sink into the preoccupied self-absorbed melancholy that submerged him entirely during his last days. His stoop and uncertain gait were already worsening. His halitosis was not so pronounced then but even so it was hard to imagine his vigorous young mistress wanting to make love with him. Yet as he declined, and as the world closed in upon him, she became more devoted. Once, when he stood in the great hall at the Berghof, dwarfed by the huge clock with the bronze eagle, she urged him to straighten himself.

'It is better for you if I stoop,' he said. 'I am as short as you then.'

'I am not short,' she protested, only half in play. 'I am

1.63 metres. That is the same as Napoleon.'

'Napoleon was taller. He was the same height as me, almost.'

'He was not. I shall prove it to you.'

For a while they were both absorbed in the search for a book that gave Napoleon's height. Edith was despatched by Eva to scour the Berghof, abandoning the letters which Eva normally insisted were to be answered within a day of receipt. But there were few books in the Berghof and none that gave Napoleon's height. The project was abandoned and Hitler sank again into the murky depths of war, the generals, the Party, the world now, the world to come and his own sense of failure. Eva was left to tittle-tattle, to entertain, to make things easy and congenial, all of which she did with a brave uncomplaining determination which Hitler never acknowledged and that Edith admired the more the more brittle with effort it became.

But when Fegelein arrived it was immediately apparent how Eva longed for attention. She flowered in his presence, her eyes brightened, her skin was softer and younger, her step quicker and yet more graceful and assured. She was as confidently flirtatious with him as he with her. Like everyone else at first, Edith assumed that it was no more than mutual and playful flirtation.

'Is he a good officer, do you think?' Eva once asked Edith when they were alone together.

'Everyone says so. Reichchancellor Himmler thinks very highly of him.'

Eva said nothing to that. After Bormann, Himmler was perhaps her least favourite man amongst the leadership. Like Bormann, he had investigated her family background once he realized how close she was to the Führer. He intercepted letters between her and her elder sister, Ilse, and between Ilse and her Italian naval officer lover. He too had referred to Eva as 'that stupid cow'. It was only with great difficulty that she had persuaded him to allow her Jewish friend, Pearl Sklar, to leave Germany. Fortunately, she had no more Jewish friends, having already dropped them.

But it was not Eva's question about Fegelein, nor their laughter, their game-playing, their obvious relish of each other's company, that had made Edith suspect there might after all be something more between them. What did it was Eva's sudden enthusiasm for making a match between her admirer and her sister, and poor Gretl's equally sudden translation in Fegelein's eyes from 'goose' to his 'sweet', his 'love'. The marriage took place eight days after the engagement. Eva intrigued, and Edith arranged, for the entire staff of the most fashionable Berlin salon to come to the Berghof to make wedding dresses. The Führer permitted the reception in the Eagle's Nest, the private retreat he had higher up the mountain than the Berghof. He even attended the wedding in Salzburg Cathedral and afterwards allowed dancing at the reception, though he did not stay for it himself. Gretl, as astonished as she was happy, was given away by Eva, not by their father, who disapproved. In her speech Eva said, 'I want this marriage to be as beautiful as if it were my own.' And then she danced with the groom.

EIGHT

Hans poured more wine, taking ceremoniously slow strides down one side of the table and back up the other. When he sat he smiled.

'No, perhaps an affair should not be described as a fact. In one sense, of course, it is a fact that it happened or did not happen, but in other senses you are right: to treat it as a mere fact would be to oversimplify a complex relation. Let me ask another question: what did you most like about her?'

'Her generosity and her bravery.'

'And what did you least like about her?'

'Her selfishness and her lack of moral imagination.'

'One may be generous and selfish?'

'Of course. The one may be a manifestation of the other.'

He pulled at the lobe of his left ear. 'Edith, what has happened to your other earring?'

'I lost it,' she said carefully. 'In that tunnel.'

'I tore them off, both of them,' she might have added, 'and held them out to the two Russian soldiers. "Take these, take these," I kept saying. "They are valuable." But we had no common language, no words at all. They knocked my hand aside. That's how I lost the other earring.'

But she said none of this. Her reference to the tunnel was a cue, had he cared to pick it up, but evidently he was not ready for that. His expression was impassive.

'Were they the earrings Eva gave you?' he asked.

'Yes, she gave them to me the day she died. She put most of her jewellery in a box and sent it to her parents in one of the last planes out of Berlin. "Something for them to live on," she said. I don't know whether it ever got there. Later, we were in the corridor in the bunker and she called me to her bedroom, which opened off the sitting room the Führer used. His own bedroom was on the other side. Traudl Junge was there already and Eva gave her her beautiful silver-fox fur coat. Traudl was on the verge of tears, although she and Eva were never very close, and kept saying, "But you will want it, you must keep it." But Eva insisted. "I always like to have well-dressed ladies around me," she said.

'And then she turned to me, took off her earrings, grabbed my hand and forced them into it, saying, "And these are for you, my dear. Keep them for me, think of me when you wear them. Or if not, use them to buy your freedom. They are very valuable. I was given them in Italy."

'I tried to refuse, to give them back to her, I pushed my hand against her but she forced my fingers closed. We were both crying. I couldn't speak. She said, "I have others that I shall wear for – when it is time. But you must wear these, for me, Edith, wear them for me." I can't remember how it ended. Someone else came into the room, I think.'

'She got them in Italy?'

Edith smiled. 'Why does that matter to you, Hans? Are you secretly a customs officer or tax inspector?'

He smiled. 'I told you. I have a passion to know.'

'She got them before the war, before I knew her. I heard about it many times.' Well, if he wanted to pursue red herrings, she was content to follow. It suited her not to be forced into making an accusation. He knew, and he knew that she knew; her reticence was her strength. If she accused him, she engaged with him; even though her accusations were just, it would mean that they engaged on the plane of assumed moral equivalence, which she was determined not to permit him.

So she told him what she had heard of the famous pre-war visit to Mussolini, when it took four special carriages to accommodate the Führer and his court. Mussolini made a great occasion of it, an operatic occasion. Edith told how Eva had laughed with the tears glistening in her eyes as she recounted – then emulated, she was a good mimic – the attempts of the leading Nazi wives to curtsy before the diminutive King Victor Emmanuel. 'The smallest king I know,' Hitler used to say whenever Victor Emmanuel was mentioned.

'You know how ungainly cows are when they lie down and get up?' Eva said. 'That is what they were like, these women, all in their dresses which had cost so much and over which they had spent weeks worrying and which were all, without exception, awful. Even Magda let herself down that time. They had no idea what to wear, what to do, their ignorance of protocol was complete – and their curtsying was so, so comic. I was nearly sick trying not to laugh.'

Edith smiled at the recollection. Hans, watchful, smiled with her. 'Eva could curtsy well,' she continued. 'She was naturally graceful and anyway she had been taught, as we all were, at our school in Munich. Her own dress sense was as good as theirs was bad and she was, of course, younger and more attractive. Despite having no official position in the Führer's court, no place in the hierarchy, no explanation for why she was there and who she was, not even permitted to appear in public, she was the centre of attention. The chief of police – an impossibly elegant man, I saw the photographs – said on meeting her that he would never have credited the Führer with such good taste. Eva loved Italy; she brought back lots of leather things – including an alligator handbag – and sacks of jewellery and she danced with Italian officers until dawn. The next night, when the Führer demanded she be back at a decent hour, she said, 'I will be back at a decent hour when you stop holding hands with Italian madonnas at the Grand Hotel.'

'She could hold her own with him, then.'

'Later, after the war started, in 1940 I think, she returned to Rome and Florence with her mother and Gretl and came back with six suitcases of clothes and thirty-seven pairs of shoes. They all smoked and drank and danced as much as they liked. When they came back through the German customs, the officials challenged her right to bring all these things into the country. She tried to explain but they were quite unsympathetic. So she rang the Führer and put the chief official on to him. She had never seen a face change so quickly, she said.'

'Where did she get the money?'

'There were similar occasions in Berlin. Once she bought one of every piece of lingerie in a dress shop. Another time she was choosing a handbag and the assistant said it would be too expensive for her. She was so annoyed she bought everything in the window and ordered it to be delivered to the Chancellery, with the bill to go to the Führer's private secretary. It was all delivered that afternoon, with flowers.'

'She was extravagant, then. Was that also a manifestation of her generosity?'

His heavy irony irritated her. 'She had an allowance of money. I don't know how much. I don't know whether she knew. Or whether she knew where it came from – the Führer himself, the Party, or the state or government. State and government were, of course, the same so far as the National Socialists were concerned, just like the Communists they hated. The Party was given money in the early days by wealthy supporters, and later took it as bribes, but most of it was simply stolen. Like the paintings in the Berghof and the gold and silver and plate. Repossessed, they called it, but it was often stolen by the SS from Jewish people. Eva had no money of her own at all but she had access to untold wealth so long as the Führer agreed, and he wasn't interested. Bormann once tried to stop her money. Apart from their being natural enemies, he never forgave her for joining with Speer to persuade the Führer that Frau Hess should not be punished after her husband fled to England.'

'To Scotland.'

'Do you remember how she and Bormann were known as the Führer's master and mistress? Perhaps you don't.'

'You forget I wasn't quite in your exalted circles. I was in charge of guards. I came and went. We weren't privy to that kind of gossip.'

'Well, in front of him they always had to get on, as I said, but in reality it was a fight to the death. She may have died first but she never lost a battle to him. When Bormann tried to stop her allowance she had all her dress bills sent to him and then told the Führer that he was using Party funds to buy clothes for his mistress. The Führer disapproved of marital irregularities and demanded to see the accounts. Bormann did not dare tell him what Eva had done, partly because he really was buying clothes for his mistress and partly because he could not risk saying anything against Eva to the Führer. And so Eva's allowance continued.'

'But still she betrayed him.'

'It depends how you define betrayal.'

'I define it in the Judas sense.'

A brave thing to say, she thought, for him of all people. Perhaps he was coming to the point. She knew she was talking more rapidly and freely than for many years, probably not since her later interrogations when she found herself wanting to go on and on talking. But was she doing it now because she, like Hans, was avoiding an essential point? Or even she rather than Hans? His questions had awoken her memories of what had happened in that tunnel, something she never usually thought about though it was always there, in the bottom drawer of her mind. Maybe she talked so freely about everything else in order not to talk about that. But it was he who should be addressing it.

She went on, telling him how Eva had persuaded Hitler not to flood the Berlin tunnels, home by then to thousands

of refugees and wounded. She told him how Eva had con-
spired with SS General Berger to frustrate Hitler's order to
kill 35,000 prisoners-of-war if the Western Allies refused to
grant a truce. The prisoners were to be taken to the moun-
tains south of Munich and shot. Eva, discovering from
Berger that he would refuse to carry out the order, arranged
that Hitler signed the orders with just the two of them present, so that there was no Bormann, nor any other
conscientious official, to check on progress. With the war
cascading towards its end, Hitler simply forgot to ask about
it. She also told him how Eva arranged for Hitler's favourite
apple-peel tea to be laced with wine, how she bleached her
medium-blonde hair to make it lighter, then tinted it to make
it darker, then once had it upswept as was then the fashion,
promptly changing it back again after Hitler said, 'You look
completely strange, completely changed to me. You are a
completely different woman.'

Without pause and without waiting for him to ask, she
described Eva's quarters in the Berghof. Adjoining Hitler's,
she had a sitting room, a dressing room, a marble bath provided by Mussolini and silk hangings on her bedroom walls.
One wall had a painting of a nude woman, supposedly her,
facing on the other a photograph of Hitler. Hitler's room,
which Edith had entered only once, was large though less
luxurious, with two tables, an easy chair, a desk beneath
bookshelves, and a wide iron-framed bed covered by a

brown quilt and a huge Swastika. Hitler wore a matching silk dressing gown and pyjamas with a black Swastika on a red background on the pocket. When, very soon after Gretl and Fegelein's wedding, the Western Allies invaded Europe, Hitler was woken with the news and left his bedroom without getting dressed. Eva stopped him from going downstairs, saying, 'Du, on this important day of your life, it would not be right for the greatest man in the world to be seen wearing his nightclothes!'

Eventually Edith stopped. Hans continued smiling but said nothing. She could no longer hear the rain but could hear, faintly, the ticking of the long-case clock in the hall. The sitting-room fire would need making up again. Hans's plate was empty, his glass almost empty. As, surprisingly, was hers. He had said he would look after the wine, but she should have noticed that he had finished his food. She should offer him more, but she sat still beneath the weight of heavy inertia. The soft light of the candles was soporific, she wanted neither to go on with the conversation nor back into her memories. His smile suggested he was still waiting for something from her. She had to force herself to speak.

'Would you like more shepherd's pie?'

'Do you think they were lovers, Eva and the Führer?'

'Of course.' The question surprised her. He raised his bushy eyebrows in query, wrinkling his forehead. 'At least, I always assumed so, didn't you?' she continued. 'Not towards the end, I suspect, given the circumstances and his decrepit state. But earlier on, surely? After all, they were together for – how many years? Fifteen or sixteen or more. It is most unlikely they would not have been lovers at some point.'

Hans shrugged, stood and poured them both more wine. 'With him, however, it is possible to imagine they were not, don't you think? In a way that it is not possible to imagine – say – Fegelein living with a young woman and not sleeping with her.'

'Possible to imagine, yes. But still, I think, earlier on . . .'

'Maybe. But there are persistent rumours and stories of his impotence, of his taste for masochistic practices, for humiliation and so on. It is possible also to imagine a far from normal sexual relationship.'

'Surely everything in sex is normal, isn't it? Including no sex. That is normal for people who really don't want it.'

'And he was married to Germany, as he always said. His mission was his bride. His unending desire for power could have been compensation for a thwarted sex life, his absolutism and assertiveness compensation for a secret yearning for humiliation.'

'Could have, might have, all these theories are always fanciful.' She sipped the wine. 'And the same could always be said of the opposites, with equal plausibility. They could have had a perfectly normal sexual relationship early on, followed by decline thereafter. That is normal. Does it matter what he did in bed, any of it? What matters far more is what people do outside the bedroom.'

'But it is interesting, is it not?'

'Is it?'

They looked at each other across the candles. She thought she could feel the heated air above them quivering slightly with challenge. Yet the challenge was not on the surface of the issue they were discussing.

'It comes back to what you think of the past,' he said. 'Whether it matters.'

'It matters enough to bury it. Bury it and forget it, so you can go on.' She spoke with finality. 'But in the more recent past I asked whether you would like more shepherd's pie.'

He smiled again. 'Thank you, Edith, I should like that very much. And while you are getting it I shall see to the fire.'

NINE

In the kitchen she had to kneel to take the pie out of the bottom oven and the effort to get up hurt her knees. She sighed as she put almost all of it on to his plate, saving only a spoonful for herself so that he wouldn't feel awkward. She would have liked nothing more than to give him his pie and go to bed. It was absurd to feel she was in some sort of competition with him, that there was an issue to be resolved. There was an issue, of course, but it did not have to be resolved. It was in the past. He had done what he had done, and she had been done to. What she said or did not say about it was her business. If he sought to explain himself, she would let him. But she would demand no explanation, nor give him the satisfaction of provoking one. The past was the past, nothing could change it. The rest was talk.

The kitchen clock showed it was already gone nine. When was the last train from Lewes? She should have found out so that she could have told him. He would surely have taken the hint. Perhaps he had taken a room in Shelley's hotel, unless he was presumptuous enough to expect to stay the night. He ought not to, because she hadn't so much as hinted that he could, but perhaps he would have to now. She really should have said something earlier. At least Mrs Hoath had seen to the big spare bedroom.

He was not there when she returned to the dining room, so she left the plates on the table and hurried, as fast as her knees would permit, upstairs to check the room.

She believed, without being sure, that she had probably exclaimed aloud when she saw it. Mrs Hoath was extraordinary: not only was the bed freshly and neatly made, with cover turned down, but the curtains were drawn, the bedside light was on and there was a fire laid in the grate. Such knowing presumption was remarkable, almost disagreeably so.

He was back in the dining room when she returned, carefully scrutinizing the ill-lit portrait of William in his tweed suit. 'He was a nice man, your husband?'

'Yes, he was a very decent man. A good man. An honourable man.' It sounded lukewarm. 'That means a lot,' she added inadequately.

He nodded. 'And a good father?'

'Very good. He would have liked more children, so that he could have been an even better one.'

'But you—'

'It was not possible.'

He sat and reached for his glass without raising it. 'Yes. We had no children. I never wanted them. That does not mean I should not have liked them if we had had them. I think there are many people like that. Many men, anyway.' He drank. 'You must remember Frau von Exner, the cook in the Berghof? The one who cooked the Führer the best vegetarian meals he had ever had, and who simmered bones in his vegetable soup without him knowing it? Her departure was a strange business.'

'How could you know about the bones, Hans? That was one of her secrets.'

'I have talked to everyone I could, I told you. Traudl Junge told me all about her. Frau von Exner was a very lively lady, wasn't she? Always laughing, and those dogs of hers. Attractive, too. She made you want to smile. And she would argue with the Führer. She seemed to have no fear of him. Perhaps that's why he treated her well.'

'I liked her very much. We all did. I learned to cook from her, more than from my own mother.'

'But wasn't it a scandal, the way she was treated?'

Edith was surprised. 'But she was well treated, exceptionally well.'

119

'Precisely. That is what I mean. The story, if I remember correctly, was that Bormann enquired into her background in order to establish her racial purity. One of her grandmothers turned out to have been a foundling, so it could not be established beyond doubt that she was free of tainted blood, Jewish blood. Therefore she had to go. The Führer called her in to tell her himself, which was an unusual compliment. He said that she would get some money and that her father would be safe in his university job and her family in their Vienna apartment. No one would suffer because of this unfortunate doubt about her record. He explained that he did with this with great regret – which I imagine was genuine – but she had to understand that he could not make one law for the German people and then be seen to flout it himself. So he said, apparently. He was in certain areas a man of principle, of self-denial, of rectitude, was he not?

'So she left, on a wave of goodwill and tears – Bormann apart, of course, because she had successfully resisted his earlier advances and no woman could be forgiven that. Then a while later, Traudl, her closest friend, had a letter from her saying not all was well, that the money had not come, that there was talk of her father not being able to remain in his job, that her brother might not be able to continue his studies. Then another letter, this time frantic because her father had lost his job, her brother was definitely unable to continue his medical studies and they were to be turned out of their apartment and sent to a camp. And still no money and no work. Had the Führer betrayed them?

'Traudl Junge, to her everlasting credit, was so upset by this that, suspecting the hand of Bormann, she did not pass on the news through the proper channels – Bormann, of course – but showed the letter to the Führer himself. That took some courage, don't you think? The Führer read the letter with mounting anger that his orders had been dis- obeyed, sent Frau Junge out and summoned Bormann. The Führer's rage could be heard throughout the Berghof. I was not there then but I imagine Bormann emerging red-faced and speechless. Frau von Exner's family were swiftly returned to their apartment, her brother resumed his medical studies, her father returned to his job and her promised money arrived. And so everyone was happy, except poor Martin Bormann, but he found other victims to feed his malice. Do you not see why this is a scandal, Edith?'

He gave her no time to respond, but continued with grow- ing energy. 'In the first place it is a scandal that Frau von Exner's grandmother's unknown origins should have any- thing to do with anything. That goes without saying. Except that it must not go without saying. It must be said, because otherwise we fall into the habit of ignoring it, as if it is simply the weather one expects at that time of year. Each and every time, it has to be said. Secondly, it is a scandal that everyone was so happy about it, as if Frau von Exner and her family had been saved from some purely natural disaster. No one questioned the rightness or wrongness of this extraordinary state of affairs. No one asked why such intervention by the Führer should be regarded as benign, even admirable, when it fact it is an outrage against humanity that it should be necessary at all. And finally, no one generalized, no one said, "Well, if it is appropriate for this one family to be saved from the camps – even though their blood may be tainted – why is it not appropriate for other families to be treated in this way?" Why was their fate unquestioned? You were there. You lived and breathed and ate with them. You were part of the silence. Can you answer that, Edith?'

Her weariness was no longer simply a longing for sleep. It was a deep reluctance to return, to re-engage. The effort of replying would be like lifting a very heavy blanket; it was better to lie still. But again he gave her no time.

'I understand why you may not want to answer. You were one of them, you were part of it. You may have thought these things but you dared not say them. That is entirely understandable. After all, you had before you the example of Henrietta von Schirach, a privileged house guest, daughter of Hoffmann the photographer and wife of the Gauleiter of Vienna. That is why she lived and that is why she survived her protest to the Führer one evening about the treatment of the Jews. She had seen Jewish families being herded on to trains in Holland and questioned why this should be, asking the Führer whether he was aware of the horrible ways in which Jews were treated. A natural enough question, but deeply unwise. The reaction? You were perhaps there that evening, Edith, you might have seen and felt it. Were you there?'

She nodded.

'You will know, then, that the reaction was silence, silence absolute, silence cold, silence menacing, a withdrawal of all human acknowledgement, recognition, intercourse, everything. Henrietta and her disgraced husband left and returned to Vienna, never visited the Berghof – were never mentioned – again. She was lucky to leave with her life. And nothing was ever said, absolutely nothing. Well, I am not saying that I would have done any differently. I can see why, after a little incident like that, people might be afraid to ask questions. Such fear is natural, reasonable, excusable.

'If fear it was. But is it as excusable if fear does not really come into it very much? What if the reason is that it simply does not occur to people to ask these questions? What if they are only vestigially, unconsciously aware that there is anything to be questioned? What if there is what you earlier ascribed to Eva alone, a complete failure of the moral imagination? Or of the moral will to imagine. Because that is what Eva exhibited, is it not, despite the exceptions you

123

plead on her behalf? And what of the rest of you – of us? Were we any better?'

Edith had to struggle to separate the questions from the questioner. The former were reasonable, the latter not. What right had he to ask her, having done what he did? It was true that he had not been often in the Berghof but he had frequently been in the bunker, where such questions were equally valid. And he had done the things he did. He should be questioning himself. He would earn the right to question others only if he had first done that. But his questions deserved answers, even if he did not. She took a deep breath and heaved back the blanket.

'All right,' she said, with a sudden surge of energy that surprised her, 'maybe we were all guilty of not asking, not daring, not thinking, not imagining. It was fear, if we had thought about it, but we did not. We were all in a cocoon, physically and mentally. We ate well, drank well, had luxuries and saw nothing of the consequences of war, the Führer least of all. Even when it was obvious that we were losing, it was until the very last days impossible to admit it to oneself. It was impossible because we could not acknowledge it between ourselves, to each other. Things only become real to us when we can speak them. Until then, no matter how real they are in fact – the house might be on fire, for example – if we are unable to admit to each other that the house is on fire we will continue to act as if it is not. Even while we burn. And we could not acknowledge those things because the Führer would not admit them. The intensity of his conviction, his passion, his delusion that the world was as he insisted it must be, was so great that it inhibited one's own judgement, warped one's own view, cut off questions at their roots. He made it impossible, when you were with him, not to be part of the world he willed. Even when he was not present, his ambience dominated. We were never not in his ambience.'

She had never spoken like this, nor thought it. Yet it was not difficult. It came easily, as if words alone gave truth to the thoughts they expressed. But she did not feel she had suffered years of frustrated expression, or relieved that she had got something off her chest. She felt liberated, without ever having felt unfree. She was no longer weary.

'We did not even ask ourselves whether we liked or admired him. We simply accepted him as Führer, as Leader. He seemed as far beyond normal human reactions as questioning a natural element, or planet. Questions were simply not appropriate, not even at the end when he was a physical and mental wreck, trembling and stinking. But you know all this. You were there too, Hans.'

'I wanted to hear you say it.'

He had finished his shepherds pie, leaving his knife and fork precisely aligned on the clean plate. She had left her spoonful untouched. They sat for a while without speech.

She heard again the faint rattling of the windows in the sitting room. The wind must have got up. He looked at her across the candles and she at him. She felt no strain. She didn't mind whether they continued or not. She was still determined not to give him the satisfaction of pressing him.

'There's cheese,' she said eventually. 'That's all.'

He inclined his head. 'I like English Cheddar particularly.'

There was only Cheddar, and not much of it. She took a slither for herself to keep him company, giving him the rest. The biscuits were stale but he either didn't notice or was too polite to say. She nibbled at hers and then did something she had not done for many years; dipped it into her wine. She was beginning to feel chilly. They should move to the sitting room soon.

'But those Jewish people,' he said. 'Do you feel any guilt about that?'

'Calling them "those Jewish people" makes it sound as if you don't.'

'Perhaps it does, as if I don't care, or even as if I am trying to suggest that we make rather too much fuss about the genocide that was attempted upon them. After all, they were not the first to suffer this and there were other races with whom it was more successful. How many Incas do we meet?' He smiled and shrugged. 'But that is not what I mean, I am not saying that. What I mean is, does it make sense to feel guilt about a terrible thing in the past which was either not one's fault at all, or in which one only had a tiny, negligible part, and over which one had absolutely no control? One might perhaps have refused to go on passively accepting it, or even – if one were very brave or stubborn – have voiced one's dissent. But one would have suffered grievously for that, not only oneself but one's family, and no judges sitting comfortably and safely in the future have the right to demand that the actors of the past should have martyred themselves and their children.

'And so I contend it does not make sense to feel personally guilty about such a thing, no matter how terrible. But many people do, not so much because they did anything, as because they were there. They feel guilt by contamination. The blood splashed on them, too. They could reasonably argue that the price of intervention would have been their own blood, but they don't, they feel guilty, as if they also murdered who only stood and watched. So they say nothing. Do you feel this guilt, Edith?'

'No.'

'Have you ever felt it?'

'No.'

'Because it is the past and the past is water under the bridge?'

'Because we were all caught up in it without fully appreciating what it was and because we were victims, too, some of us.' She paused. 'And because we knew many others who were also victims.'

He made no reaction.

'You might say we should have understood what was happening,' she continued, 'and should now feel guilty that we did not. I might agree, but still not feel genuinely guilty because I am human, fallible, fallen, limited, subject to a confined generosity. I may admit guilt without feeling it. Do you feel any guilt, Hans?'

'Not about that.'

That was the nearest he had come to an admission. She waited to see if he went on, but he did not. They moved to the sitting room, where he again rearranged the logs and poked the fire with needless thoroughness. She brought him coffee and herself tea.

'Unless you wish to find an hotel in Lewes, or have already booked one, you are going to have to stay the night,' she said.

He straightened slowly, poker in hand. 'Do you know, I have not even thought about it? Extraordinary. It is most kind of you.' He smiled.

She did not believe him.

'Fegelein would have felt no guilt,' he continued, still holding the poker. 'He was not capable of it.'

'No, but I'm sure he could feel shame, humiliation, especially public humiliation. Perhaps not personal guilt because that implies responsibility to others, or at least to something beyond yourself.'

'And fear, at the end. He begged for mercy.'

'Begging for mercy may be the most sensible thing to do, especially when it is the only thing left.'

'I didn't see it all. I was in and out of the bunker, as you know. Tell me how it went with him at the end.'

'You know what happened to him, Hans. You just like getting people to tell you things, don't you? Maybe you just like stories. Is there anyone you are not interested in?'

'Only the Führer himself. He was not interesting because he was mad, even by your definition which has Magda Goebbels as sane. That is, if I understand it, an inability to perceive realities?'

She smiled. 'I suppose so. Except that that makes us all mad, at different times.'

'Yes, but he was consistently so. You recall the end of his extraordinary wedding at two in the morning, with that terrified Herr Wagner hauled out of bed to perform the ceremony in the bunker during the shelling and bombing? Several times Eva had to say to him, "Herr Wagner, can we get on with the ceremony? It is getting late." And at the end, during that sad little party, more like a wake, there was a big bomb that shook white flakes from the ceiling down upon them, like confetti. Confetti for the damned, for the doomed. And then the Führer made a speech about retiring and settling down in Linz, his birthplace, as an "average citizen". You could never have imagined that. That was madness, to believe for one second that such a life was possible for him. Only someone with no awareness of what he had done and was continuing to do could possibly have said such a thing. It showed that this man was fundamentally disconnected from the realities within which most of us live most of the time.'

He stood before her, staring, poker in hand. 'You cannot follow people into madness, Edith.'

TEN

At that moment Edith could not bring herself to look into his eyes. She stared instead into the fire. It was absurd to fear that he might be about to batter her with the poker, quite absurd, but she preferred not to look.

'You don't know where the mad are,' Hans continued, as if musing aloud. 'Or where they are going. You don't know what they see, hear, perceive. It's madness that is another country, not the past, as your writer said. Contrary to what is widely assumed, the mad are less interesting than the rest of us, not more. The sane are more interesting because we see how they cope or fail to cope with our shared realities. Fegelein, for instance, a flawed character, a very limited soul, was not mad. He saw things as the rest of us saw them. That was evident in how he tried to negotiate them, to turn them to his advantage, however obviously and finally fruitlessly. They were lovers, surely, he and Eva? They must have been, despite what you say about the ambiguity of affairs.' He dropped the poker with a clatter on to the stone hearth and returned to his sofa.

As she felt her body relax she realized how stiffly she had been holding herself, and hoped he hadn't noticed. 'I believe not.'

One of the logs was hissing. As she stared at it a spark shot on to the faded carpet. The carpet had suffered this many times over many years. It had been beautiful and was probably still valuable. In earlier years she would have hastened to put it out but now she found herself reflecting that there were other things in life, even if no longer very many of them. After a few moments she stretched out her foot to the spark, couldn't quite reach it, decided against getting up, then smiled her thanks as Hans heaved himself out of the sofa he had just settled in and came across and stamped on it, although by then it was out. He lowered himself back on to the sofa, his face red and his bow tie askew. He was a little breathless.

'I didn't recall that you were at the wedding,' she said.

'I wasn't really, I was along the corridor, but there was some signal or other so I came along at the end. You told me about it afterwards.'

'Did I?' She didn't remember that, either. Events had moved very quickly afterwards. She sipped her tea. 'I disagree about the Führer. I think he was not mad and was interesting. All of us have escapist fantasies like Linz but they don't signify madness. He perceived what we perceived, only he insisted on bending the world to his will. I imagine that's what many criminals try to do. At first, when he was successful, it must have seemed to him that he really could do it. Later, as it became increasingly clear he couldn't, he raged like a spoilt child and blamed everyone but himself – the Army, the Navy, the Luftwaffe, the generals, the Party, the Jews, the English and Americans, the Russians, the German people, history, fate, God Himself if he could have believed in Him. He was obsessed but not mad. What he said was entirely understandable, his views and attitudes were consistent and predictable, you could follow his thoughts, you could anticipate them. To write him off as mad is to relegate him to another sphere, to refuse to understand, to refuse to accept that he was like us, one of us. That is why he was so dangerous and why it is so dangerous not to acknowledge him. It makes it more possible for it to happen again.'

He held up his hands. 'All right, we will leave the Führer. But tell me, why do you say that Eva and Fegelein were not lovers?'

She sighed. 'Think about it.'

'Think about what it was like for us,' she might have said. 'You showed interest, you courted me almost, but you couldn't have seduced me even if I had been willing, as perhaps I was. It was impossible to be alone in that place.'

Instead, she continued: 'How, when and where could they have done it? Not in the Berghof. There was plenty of room, certainly, and they would have had plenty of time, but there were staff everywhere and the routine of the house was such that everyone always knew where everyone was. You must remember that. Certainly, I always knew where Eva was. I was supposed to, I had to, it was my job to know, she wanted me to know so that I could do things for her. She was always summoning me for this or that and if it wasn't me it was her hairdresser or Gretl or her maid or someone. She had her own little court, she was no solitary flower, she neither needed nor sought privacy, still less solitude. She could not be herself when she was alone because there was no single self for her to be. She became herself only with others, in a social context, and which self she became depended on who they were and on what they expected. She simply became whatever they expected. This is what made and unmade her. If she had been born in England she would have adored Mr Churchill.

'And a clandestine affair in the bunker would have been quite impossible. You remember how crowded it was there, how you were never, ever alone. Admittedly, she and the Führer had their own rooms – they alone – but you had to walk through the Führer's busy room to get to them. It would have been impossible to smuggle anyone in or out. And Fegelein's quarters, wherever they were, could have been no more private than yours. A bunk in a tunnel, probably.'

Again he shook his head before she finished speaking. It irritated her. 'But Eva was in the bunker only for the last few days,' he said, 'and for months before that Fegelein was often away, travelling between the Führer and Himmler. They could have met in Munich when she visited her parents or friends – she had a house there, remember, given her by the Führer – or anywhere else they could both find reason to be. In fact, how did she get to the bunker? There were no trains by then. Who brought her there? Fegelein?'

'Another SS officer, Walter Galen. I was with her in Munich and he picked us up in the black Mercedes she had at her disposal. We had both been to visit our parents. Munich was awful, so much destruction, everywhere the smell of burning and sewers, and everywhere homeless, hungry, people.' She thought again of Hans's dead sister. 'Well, I don't need to tell you what it was like. It's a long drive anyway to Berlin but it was even longer because of road damage, detours, the need to find fuel, army convoys, all the tedium and drudgery of war. Three times we were strafed by English aeroplanes. The first time they hit an army lorry in front that blew up in a great ball of flame, so hot we could feel it in the car even though we were not very close. The second plane came around again but Galen stopped the car beneath a viaduct and we were saved. Later we were attacked again and one of our tyres was shot and burst but Galen drove us into a wood where we stayed until about three in the morning. He had to change the wheel. We waited a long time there because we were not far from Berlin and could see it was suffering a big night raid. We could hear the crump-crump and see the flames and the red glow against the clouds. We continued when we thought the raid was finished but as we were going through the suburbs it started again and we had to go into a public shelter. That was awful, a glimpse – and smell – of hell, horribly crowded, frightened and desperate people, children wailing, mothers with babies, no water, no lavatories, no fresh air. We never spoke about it after we came out. Outside was almost as bad, with trees across the roads, and great holes filled with water. But Eva was determined to get to the bunker, simply determined.'

'Because Fegelein was there?'

'When we arrived the Führer was sitting on the blue and white striped sofa in his study, the one they died on. He had forbidden her to join him in the bunker but when he saw her he pushed himself to his feet with trembling arms and said, "I told you to go to the Berghof. It is . . ." but he could not finish. They held hands and for the next few hours sat on the sofa together talking about old happy times, looking at photographs and listening to records on that record player. They were like a sentimental old couple, or as if she were a fond daughter visiting her father in an old people's home. I do not believe she went there for Fegelein.'

'But he was there, wasn't he? They danced at that party on the Führer's birthday. I was there for a short while. So were you. I was going to ask you to dance but I was summoned away. And they had danced together before, at the Berghof. She was obviously drawn to him. You just had to see them together, what is now called their body language.'

Edith nodded. 'Yes, and in another world she might have been his conquest and he hers. They could have been very bad for each other, or very good. Probably bad, given how these things usually work out.'

'Tell me how it ended.'

'You know all that. We talked about it at the time.'

'Perceptions differ, memory is unreliable.'

'Fegelein went missing. That is, he was not around for a while. That was not unusual because he had to liaise with Himmler who was always away. Eva was trying to take the Führer's mind off depressing things such as – well, such as everything, I suppose – but really off their approaching end. I think she was trying to take her own mind off it, too. Hitler had already given us the potassium cyanide suicide pills that Himmler and his SS had developed, and presumably tested thoroughly in the usual ways and places.'

ALAN JUDD

'What were they like, those pills?'

'Were you not issued with one? Perhaps the Army didn't get them. They were in pretty little holders, like lipstick holders, and inside was a small phial of golden liquid. You just had to pop it in your mouth and bite, Hitler told us when he handed them out at dinner. A funny time to issue them. We would die instantly, he said. He knew that because he had one tried on Blondi, his German shepherd, and it killed her straight away. It was the only time anyone saw him weep.

'Anyway, Eva was trying to persuade him to let her have a beautiful little statue that was in the Reich Chancellery gardens. She and I used to walk there every day among the shell holes and broken trees until the shelling got too bad. It was a statue of a girl. "It would look wonderful by the pool in my garden in Munich," she said to him. "Please buy it for me after we leave Berlin."

'But the Führer said it was probably state property and he couldn't take it just like that. He was often very correct about such things, so long as they didn't really matter. And then she put her hand on his arm and said, "But if you beat back the Russians and free Berlin, you can make an exception." He laughed, which was rare then, a triumph for Eva. That's how she kept things going.

'This was the kind of thing she was trying to do practically all the time. She wasn't always partying. And then two

138

things happened. I am not sure in which order, I don't think I ever knew. But this is the order in which I knew them. First Fegelein rang Eva in the bunker. He was in an apartment somewhere in Berlin and he pleaded with her to join him. "You are finished if you stay there," he said. "It is over. But we can both leave, we can both get out, we can start a new life in the West. My chief" – he meant Himmler – "is nego-tiating with the British. We have contacts. You must come with me, Eva."

'Or something like that. I did not hear it all, of course, although I was with her when the call came. When I realized what sort of conversation it was I left her alone. For days before he rang she had been asking everyone where he was, she was always looking for him. Now she kept saying into the telephone, "Where are you? Where are you?" So I grant you there was something between them, that she cared for him despite his being married to her sister, poor pregnant Gretl. He didn't ring Gretl, of course.'

Hans clenched his fists on his thighs. 'I still believe they could have had an affair. They both at least thought about it. You must admit that. At least. That is enough, isn't it?'

She looked at him. 'Why does it matter so much to you, Hans?'

'Because I don't know it for certain and I want to know, I want to be certain about everything.'

'But there are many things you don't know. Why are you

so insistent on this? It's not as if it makes any difference to anything.'

'If they did it's further evidence that everything and every-one was rotten to the core, that we were all guilty.'

'That's what you want, is it?'

He held her gaze, then smiled. 'But they did, didn't they? Surely they must've.'

She sighed again. 'If they could have found somewhere to do it and if they were burning for each other, they might have, I suppose. Not must. And not in the bunker. Anyway, I don't know how the call ended but then the second thing happened, though it may have happened already: Hitler was informed of Himmler's attempts to negotiate with the English. It was broadcast on the radio. Hitler was in a great rage because he thought Himmler had betrayed him. "Mein treue Heinrich," he kept saying, "Mein treue Heinrich." He wanted Fegelein immediately, so an SS search party was sent to find him. Günsche somehow knew where the apartment was. It must have been quite nearby because most of Berlin was in Russian hands by then. They found him drunk, with a red-headed girl who escaped through the window. I wonder who she was and what happened to her.' She stared into the fire. 'When they brought him back Hitler said he was to be court-martialled for deserting his post and stripped of his rank and sent to join the soldiers defending Berlin.

'But then they searched his briefcase and found foreign currency and documents about Himmler's negotiations. The Führer was even more furious. He shouted that this was treachery and that Fegelein must be shot. Eva wept when she heard. She was distraught, whether for herself or Gretl or both I don't know. After Fegelein was court-martialled, which happened in the upper bunker somewhere, they let him send her a note which said something like, "Eva, tell the Führer I am innocent. Beg him for a reprieve for me until I can prove my innocence, please. I am in the Reich Chancellery garden under guard." She went to the Führer and begged for Fegelein's life, but he became angry with her – the only time I knew him angry with her – and shouted, "We can't allow family affairs to interfere with disciplinary action. Fegelein is a traitor just as Mussolini's son-in-law was a traitor, and you know what happened to him." Eva had liked Mussolini's son-in-law and had asked Hitler to intervene on his behalf but he was executed by Mussolini. She sent a reply to Fegelein which took a long time to write, even though it simply said, "I can do nothing." She did not sign it. She sat staring at it for a long time. Then she gave it to me to send. I imagine she could think of nothing else to say that was neither trite nor futile nor dangerous. What do you say? Do you sign it with little kisses or write, "Love, Eva"? The man is about to die. She told him the only thing that mattered.

'It was before midnight when he was court-martialled. About an hour and a half afterwards he was shot in the garden next to the statue Eva wanted. About an hour and a half after that Hitler married Eva. One day and a half later they were both dead.'

Edith finished her lukewarm tea and poured herself another. Her recitation had been matter-of-fact, as if so well rehearsed that she no longer had any interest in herself and did it without thinking. In fact, she had never described those events before and, as she did so, they were present to her in vivid, unsequential flashes of irrelevant detail – the light blue edging on the handkerchief Eva used to dry her eyes, the tiny food stains on the Führer's grey jacket when he came into the corridor after shouting at Eva, pale and still visibly angry, the unceasing hum of the diesel generators, Eva's frank, frail, determined, dry-eyed expression as she handed Edith her note to Fegelein and said, 'Please ask that this is put in his hand.'

Yet when she told it, it was different. The recitation of events never conveyed their feel, their smells, their sounds and associations. These were irrelevant to factuality, to sequential ordering, to cause and effect, all the necessary qualities for a true understanding of the past. That was why even the truest accounts of the past were inadequate and why the past was not worth bothering with, except as a record. One had to get on with things as they were now and not bother with what had been. Yet still most vividly of all she recalled the desperate gaiety of the dance on Hitler's birthday, when Fegelein lifted Eva above his head and lowered her the length of his body, their eyes locked, her skirt caught up unheeded. That memory had often come unbidden to her over decades. No one had ever done that to her. She had so wanted, she acknowledged to herself only now, to be Eva at that moment. To her great surprise, she still did.

ELEVEN

Hans finished his coffee. He looked as if he wanted another. 'I still don't understand why you are so interested in all this,' she said. 'You were there. You know at least half of whatever I can tell you. You say the study of the past helps us to understand the present but nothing I have told you, or can tell you, contributes anything to our understanding of our world today, or of ourselves. And why have you waited until now, when we are both nearly dead?'

'I have not waited until now. I told you I have talked to everyone I could find. You are the last.'

She leaned forward. 'Why Hans? Why?'

'May I have some more coffee?'

He began his struggle to get up from the sofa but she got up first, took his cup, filled it and handed it back to him. For a moment she was tempted to sit on the sofa with him, as if closing to her target, but he might mistake that for friend-ship. She resumed her own seat and her own tea.

'It is my passion,' he said.

'It is not a passion. It is more like pornography.'

He smiled. 'Past-porn. Yes. It has something of the same obsessional quality as pornography, and perhaps some of the same limitations. You do not respond to it fully, only with a part of yourself. It is vicarious. You seek to evoke it for yourself through the eyes of others. You seek their experi-ence without their responsibility.'

'But you were there. If there is responsibility, you share it.'

His Adam's apple bobbed vigorously. 'Of course, of course, I do not deny my own part in all this. But I was only intermittently there, as you know, being based mainly in the Chancellery.'

'What happened to KK?' He looked at her. 'Your friend, Kurt Kelter,' she prompted. 'You can't have forgotten him. You were inseparable, almost.'

He laughed. 'Of course, of course, I haven't heard anyone call him that for years. He died in the camps, in Russia. We were never in the same one. But, tell me, what became of you, what happened to you afterwards, before you were captured by the British?'

She stared. 'What happened to me?'

'Yes, during the breakout and afterwards, when we all left. Can you still remember it and describe it?'

The fire spat a shower of sparks, one again landing on the carpet. Again, she disregarded it until it had done its damage, and only then moved her foot across to the little blackened spot. She was more worried about her dress than the carpet, and more struck by his question than by anything else he could have said.

'Why do you wish me to describe it, Hans?'

He looked awkward and embarrassed, but also excited and nervous. Well he might, she thought.

'I wish to hear it in your own words,' he said carefully.

This was pornography, surely. She debated with herself whether to participate in it with this dinner-jacketed old man, a stranger to her now, at best a curiosity. Why should she indulge his lust for the detritus of the past? Or help him ease his own guilt by vicariously participating in that of others? If they were all guilty, he could persuade himself that his own was less – was that how it worked with him? And if they felt no guilt he would argue that they should. In which case, why get her to recount the one episode in which guilt was indisputably his, and his alone?

She had never talked about it, never, and she tried never to think about it. Yet she felt the guilt of it almost as if she had done what he had done. Guilt by association, guilt by con-tamination.

'Has the rain stopped?' she asked.

They listened. There was nothing apart from the ticking of the hall clock and the sounds of the fire.

'Why, were you thinking we might take another walk, Edith?' His manner was suddenly winsome, almost comically suggestive.

'I was thinking of our walk through Berlin. That night walk.'

It began in the bunker, the night following the deaths of Hitler and Eva. Their suicides proved infectious; not only the Goebbels family but two generals and various others, not only in the Führerbunker but throughout the population of the Chancellery bunkers. Like Magda Goebbels, they despaired of a world without National Socialism, a world without cause or meaning. Only, unlike Magda, they decided for themselves alone, not for their children. Except for one of the doctors, she learned later. He had gathered his unsuspecting family together for what was to be their last meal, then detonated grenades beneath the table.

They thought they were protecting their children, she supposed, not only from life without the Leader but from Russian rape and brutality. Well, there had been enough of that, God knew. But it was random and arbitrary. Although terrifying and unpredictable, the arbitrariness meant that most survived. She had reason to be grateful for that. Those Nazi children would probably have survived their Soviet orphanages to find a world without National Socialism not quite as unendurable as their parents anticipated. They would be grandparents now.

For herself, there had been no question of suicide. While the Führer lived, his presence had been protective, paternal, even – sometimes – kindly. His relentless passion had stifled their own real emotions and natural feeling in those around him, absorbing them into himself, taking them over, converting them into his own currency and leaving them with nothing of themselves. Hence Magda, mother of six, had no feelings left to call her own, only worship for the man who gave her what she had always yearned for: a cause to believe in, something to be passionate about. And so, living a husk of a life that was no longer fully her own, she had denied life to her children.

In Edith, however, Hitler's death provoked a fierce desire to live, a determination to survive born of youthful optimism and a reawakened sense of herself. She was angry with him for what felt like desertion, an abdication of responsibility. Surviving thus became a refutation of him. For a while she did not even think about Eva.

She did not hesitate to join those planning to break out of the bunker that night. It was unlikely to work, said Günsche, but it was better to try their luck than to die like rats in a cellar. She left the bunker without emotion. Even the sight of her clothes and small possessions abandoned in the room she shared with three other girls moved her not at all.

Without that which had given it a kind of life, at least an intensity, the bunker was just a sordid, smelly, noisy place. It was good to leave. Traudl Junge left Eva's silver-fox fur coat in the corner, but Edith wore Eva's earrings. She also wore the thin gold ring her mother had given her when she left home. Such things might be useful for barter in days to come.

Before leaving she and Traudl crept into the Führer's sitting room where it had all ended. The doors were open; quite suddenly, no one was interested in anything to do with Hitler. Indifferent to what had happened to him and to what he had stood for, they were already looking out only for themselves. Edith and Traudl trod gingerly, as if on broken glass rather than carpet. The scene was as she later described to William, though in recalling it now she realized she must have noticed more detail than she had recounted. From the door they could see blood on one end of the sofa, on the wall behind it, and on the floor. There was a pistol on the floor. At the other end of the sofa, placed carefully together on the carpet, were Eva's white cork shoes that she had worn for her wedding. On the low table in front was the small pistol she had owned but never used, next to her pink chiffon scarf. On the floor, glinting in the electric light, was the brass case of the potassium cyanide capsule. On the coat stand hung Hitler's grey overcoat with the gold national emblem, his cap with his pale suede gloves folded on it, and

Blondi's lead. There was the strong smell of bitter almonds she had emphasized to William. The sight of Eva's scarf and her neat shoes – she sat on the sofa with her feet tucked under her – brought tears unexpectedly to Edith's eyes, but not for long. 'I want to be a pretty corpse,' Eva had said. Now she was ashes.

They did not linger. Although it was warm, Edith took her coat – something to sleep under at night – and, on Günsche's advice, no money but as many cigarettes as she could find and cram into the pockets. At about eight-thirty in the evening the first group gathered. There was a number of soldiers, led by the bunker guard commander and Günsche, and four girls. They left the Führerbunker through narrow crowded passages that Edith had never seen before, connecting with the network of shelters and bunkers beneath the Reich Chancellery. As they went higher they had to scramble through holes in walls, slipping and grazing themselves on the rubble of shattered staircases before eventually gathering in a large coal cellar with another group of escapees, which included Hans. He it was, she recalled, who found army clothes for the girls – trousers, jackets, boots, steel helmets.

'When we get out there it is important not to stand out,' he said. 'Look like us, be anonymous. We will tear off our badges of rank and declaration. And wear these but use them only if you have to.' He handed out belts weighed down with pistols in holsters. 'They are already loaded. We have no more ammunition, so save a bullet for yourselves.' When he came to Edith he smiled and lowered his voice. 'Stay with me. I will look after you.'

She felt uncomfortable that he should single her out from Traudl and the others, but she nodded acceptance. 'I will look after you, Edith,' he repeated. He had always called her 'Fräulein' in company before.

The army clothes, particularly the boots and helmet, felt heavy and cumbersome. They seemed to resist the wearer, taking no cognizance of individuality nor of softer female flesh and lighter bones. Her helmet lurched painfully backwards and forwards on her head and her boots made every step a conscious clumping effort. She was grateful for the disguise, however, when they passed through a wide subterranean chamber that had become an operating theatre. She had never before seen dead bodies, nor the grievously wounded, nor great quantities of blood, let alone buckets of feet, hands, bits of limbs and other less identifiable parts. Nor had she experienced such stench, heat, groans and screams. Hans led them as if wading through refuse. She followed his broad shoulders, focusing on them, content for her helmet to hide her. She could not imagine how the nurses stayed.

Then somehow they were in the underground railway system, again stepping over bodies, this time mostly clothed and alive. The stench was different but no less potent. Thousands were sheltering from the shelling and firing above, which was nearer and louder now. The glances that fell upon them were no longer suffering or pleading but passive, exhausted, dull, listless, some resentful, a few hostile. Their purposeful progress, uniforms and weapons protected them. Again she was careful to look neither to the right nor to the left.

'But I don't need to rehearse all this for you,' she said to Hans. 'I was literally following your footsteps.'

'I had forgotten the hospital. Isn't that strange? Now that you mention it, it comes back most vividly but if I had been asked to give an account I should have not have mentioned it.' He smiled. 'That shows why remembering needs to be collaborative.'

'Have I left anything out so far?'

'You could not have remained in army clothes. You must have changed somewhere. Where was that?'

'You must remember. It was the next day, in a shed, some kind of workshop, where we spent the rest of the night. We were out of the underground system and we had crossed streets, near Chausseestrasse I remember for some reason, and then we had had to hide from the Russian tanks. Some of our party had separated by then. We just lay down on the dirt floor and slept. The next day sometime we met some Yugoslav men with whom we exchanged cigarettes for food and they told us that we girls would be safer dressed as ordinary civilians now with nothing to hide. It was better for the men to stay as soldiers. You told us we must find women's clothes.'

'Where did you find them?'

'You found them.'

'Me?' He put his finger to his chest, eyebrows raised. 'Are you sure it was me?'

She smiled. 'Hans, you surely cannot have forgotten that you went out and found a looted lingerie shop and came back with your gun and your helmet festooned with dirty bras and knickers you had found trodden into the floor? Everybody laughed. It was the only time.'

He looked slightly embarrassed, which made her smile again. He had looked embarrassed then, when they had all laughed.

'And then you went out again,' she continued, 'and returned with old skirts, dresses, pullovers, shirts, coats, filthy old clothes that had probably been abandoned by female looters who had found better. We put those on, horrible though they were, except there weren't enough coats or jackets so I kept my army jacket because I needed something extra at night, although I abandoned my army coat for a fashionable high-shouldered one that was too big. I still have it. I shouldn't have kept the army jacket, of course, but we were not always quite logical then, we

153

were not thinking clearly. We were exhausted, I suppose.'

'It suited you, Wehrmacht uniform.'

'It did nothing of the kind. You are romanticizing. More than that, fantasizing. This is more pornography, Hans. There was nothing remotely romantic or attractive in Berlin in May 1945. Everything was awful. Everything. You know that.'

He nodded. 'That is why we must relive it. That is how we come to terms with past awfulness. We have to bring it to the surface, admit it, discuss it, let it out. That way we dispel its poison, the harm evaporates, it no longer inhibits or imprisons us, we are free to go forward. Repressed horrors are spiritually and emotionally cancerous, they turn against their host and destroy you. Always, always we must set them free, and so free ourselves of them.'

'Claptrap.'

She spoke sharply. The word reverberated like a slap in the silence that followed. A tension arose between them. She needed no one, she felt, to lecture her on how to deal with her own past. Least of all Hans. Different people had different ways of coping. For some, talking about it was a way of dealing with it, for the reasons he had given. For others, repression or suppression – at least not dwelling on it, not thinking about it – was the way the skin healed. Perhaps it was different for different people at different times. It was often said that hers was the last generation to display the famous English stiff upper lip, but to her mind it was neither exclusively English nor always stiff. Nor was it simply a question of generations. It was having to cope with things, things that don't simply happen once or happen for a while and then stop, leaving you more or less intact and free to talk about them afterwards and so make yourself feel better. Rather, it was how you had to be when you had to cope with things that went on and on and on, like grinding poverty and war. If you wanted to survive you had to go on with them, and go on coping. And you did that not by going on about it but by getting on with it. If you went on about them, you wouldn't cope. She had seen it in her parents' generation, in the men who returned from the trenches and the women who survived near starvation at home. Mostly they did not talk about it, unless to those who had shared it. She had seen it again in her own generation, and in herself. True, it was not good to pretend things had never happened, but neither was it good to go on serving them up for dinner. That suggested an unhealthy appetite.

But she wanted to show no more of her resentment than she had already. It was like allowing him to see he had got through, that he had scored a hit. She tried to appear conciliatory. 'You say this, Hans, and it is true that many other people also say it. It is a contemporary orthodoxy and doubtless it works for some. Yet you do not practise it yourself. You say nothing about what you felt, what happened to you. You ask me, you asked others. For yourself, you seem to practise what I preach.'

'Voyeurism, I am a voyeur, is that what you are saying?' He smiled unconvincingly. 'You may be right.'

She returned to her silence. Such apparently simple candour was too calculated, too pat, too self-conscious, too easy. She no longer minded being silent. When she was young she had a horror of silences and used to leap in to fill them, fill them with anything, but now, if there was nothing she wanted to say, she said nothing. Although surprised by the strength of her resentment and mistrust of him, she was not sufficiently interested in him, nor in herself, to analyse it. What did it matter if he was putting on an act, or if he indulged this suspect lust of his? What had happened had happened and nothing now could alter it. What did it matter that they were the two last beings on earth to have lived this particular past? Their eyes alone had seen Hitler and Eva at the end, their ears alone knew the precise timbre of Eva's tinkling voice, the softness of Hitler's in private. Her hands, her once shapely hands, were now perhaps the only living hands to have touched both of theirs. Her lips were surely the last living lips to have kissed Eva's. She almost felt them now, that fleeting softness, a brush, the lightest touch, yet a statement. Of what? Farewell? Remember me? Thank you? I am frightened – comfort me?

'It is raining again now,' he said.

She realized she had been hearing it without noticing. The draught moved the curtains uneasily. It was easy to imagine why people believed in ghosts. Rain was doubtless seeping through on to the floor again. The fire had burnt low. She did not stir to see to it. She still said nothing.

'Is there brandy?' he asked.

She had to think. Of course there was – must be – but no one had drunk it since William was alive. No – Michael at Christmas, he must have, surely. She would get more in for next Christmas. She liked to see Michael comfortable, with a glass of something after dinner; it made him slow down. He was too busy, in danger of a heart attack, he ought to slow down.

She got up with a rustle of skirt and pains in her knees, and went to the drinks cupboard. That rustle reminded her of William, too, it used to excite him, that, and the susurration of silk and nylon. Knowing it excited him used to excite her too. There were two bottles of brandy, both less than half full.

'Old one or very old one?' she asked. She couldn't read the labels without her glasses.

'The elder, if I may.'

She poured from the one with less in. Then – something she hadn't done for years and years – she poured one for herself.

He sniffed and tasted it. 'A very fine brandy, Edith.'

'I am relieved.'

She sat and sipped it. The taste and smell reminded her strongly of William and tweed and the lighting of pipes after dinner. He should have been buried in tweed. 'What is it like to be dead?' she remembered asking her mother, when she was younger than her own grandchildren now. 'Like before you were born,' her mother had said.

They listened to the rain again.

'And what happened then?' he asked.

She stared. 'You know what happened.'

'I should like you to tell me.'

She continued staring. He was becoming more a stranger to her, not less. She felt she could see less and less of the old Hans in him. After all these years, of course, that should not be surprising, but his question made her feel he was more than a stranger, almost an enemy. 'You know very well what happened,' she repeated slowly.

'But I don't know all of it.'

That at least was true. His voice was cajoling, almost gentle, his face in shadow when he sat back in the sofa. There was a spot of shepherds pie on his white shirt front. Her curiosity about him resurged. What did he want, why was he doing this? It was surely more than a disinterested passion for the past, the desire of an historian manqué to fix events in which he had himself participated. It was surely more than the desire of a counsellor manqué to cure her – as he would see it – of her suppression of her own past. She didn't believe it was for her at all, nor for the sake of that past, nor for those who had peopled it. It wasn't to understand, whatever he might say. It was for himself, in some way she neither perceived nor liked. But if that was really what he wanted, then she would let him have it. See how he liked it.

TWELVE

'You will remember – or perhaps you won't – that it was decided that we women would have a better chance of escaping Berlin if we went simply as ordinary civilian refugees unaccompanied by men. The Russians, if they did not molest us, were more likely to let us through their lines than if we were with men. I say lines but, as you know, there were no lines as such. It was all much more confused than that. There were soldiers, tanks, guns, bodies, refugees, more soldiers, rubble and dust everywhere and sounds of gunfire and shellfire but you never knew where from, unless they were very close. Everything was chance, whether you lived or died, whether you received food or a fist, whether you ran into helpful compatriots or kind Russians or cruel Russians or children or unhelpful compatriots, SS diehards who hanged from lamp posts anyone they decided might be a deserter. Finding water was one of the few constants of life, something you had to do. Everything else was random or arbitrary.

'And also, of course, there was the Hitler Youth. Those boys. Remember them, Hans?' She wished she still smoked. A cigarette would have been perfect for that moment. She would have taken a long pull on it and then exhaled slowly, considering him through the smoke, observing the effects of her words as a general might observe the distant fall of his artillery shells.

The general would have been disappointed.

'Of course, yes, the Hitler Youth,' said Hans, as if reminded of the weather.

'They were so young.'

'Mere boys.'

'Not many of them.'

'Very few in Berlin.'

'Fewer still by the end.'

He nodded, gazing into his brandy, then into the fire. It was possible that he was remembering those pale little fourteen-year-olds or whatever they were, with their ill-fitting uniforms, cropped hair and expressions at once precociously brutal and childishly self-conscious. They carried their guns and anti-tank grenade launchers with such obvious pride and such unconvincing nonchalance. Confused, fanatical, loyal and lost – in every sense lost – they made her want both to flee from and to save them. Was it possible that this was how Hans remembered them?

'Of course, there were old men, too,' he said. 'Old men and boys, with nothing between. And nothing between them and the Russian tanks.' He still stared into the fire.

'Weren't they in a bomb crater at a junction, the first time we saw them?' She spoke musingly, as if she really were drawing on a cigarette between phrases. 'Three of them, by themselves, facing the way they thought the tanks would come? They stared at us as we passed. Their faces were so young, so pale. No one said anything. I suppose we just stared back, did we?'

'I don't remember.'

'It was just before we split up, the women and the men.' His studied lack of reaction made her more determined. 'There were the same ones, those three, that we saw later. You and I.'

He nodded, very slightly. She felt she had made her point. 'And so the women of our party agreed to set off together,' she continued briskly. 'Otto Günsche told us to head north towards the British lines – there were lines outside Berlin – once we had got out of the city. 'Go to the British, they will look after you,' he said. That was what Speer had said to Magda Goebbels. Well, it turned out to be true for me.

'Anyway, there was Gerda Christian, Traudl Junge,

Constanze Manziarly, the cook, and two girls I didn't know from the Chancellery. Thanks to you, Hans, we had civilian clothes except that Constanze and I still had our Wehrmacht jackets. Otto Günsche tried to persuade us to leave them but we said we would dump them as soon as we found something else, we were so afraid of being cold. Ridiculous. At that point you said you would come and help us, to set us on our way out of the city. This, of course, was directly contrary to the logic of what Günsche had said but he and everyone agreed to it; I don't think any of us was thinking straight by then. You were standing near me, looking at me, when you said you would come with us. Rightly or wrongly, I interpreted it personally. I thought you were going to look after me.'

He looked at her now, attentive, unembarrassed. He could not really have forgotten, surely? Or was his passion for the past so overriding that personal considerations were irrelevant, merely quaint as if you were looking back on life from beyond death? After waiting to see if he would say anything, she continued.

'A group of men, including Bormann, Stumpfegger – the doctor who helped poison the Goebbels children – and Kempka, the Führer's chauffeur, decided to go too, but in a different direction. At first, everything was all right with us. We were more or less ignored and hardly saw any Russians. I can't remember where we went. I barely knew the city and

I think we were all more tired than we realized. Anyway, with buildings collapsed and bomb craters in the streets and constant detours, it would have been hard to tell even if I had known it. But you said we were going in the right direction, and then someone somewhere said there was a Russian checkpoint around the next corner and that they were letting through only civilians with papers. Well, we had kept the papers that showed us as civilian employees in the Reich Chancellery, and we didn't know how they would interpret that. And you, of course, were in uniform. So we decided to try and find another way round.

'We were all hungry and thirsty and it was hot. We seemed to spend hours scrambling over bricks and concrete, picking our way through houses that had half collapsed and looking for tunnels we might use. It was very hot, I remember, and I think it was the afternoon. Was it?'

'I think it must have been.'

'Eventually we found a way round and came up near one of the bridges, I can't remember which. This was out of the frying pan and into the fire. It was a much more dangerous area, with a lot of shooting and fighting around the bridge. There was a tank on the road ahead of us, a German one, firing its gun and moving towards the bridge. Running behind it were some soldiers, keeping under cover of it. But then we realized that they weren't really soldiers but some of our other group from the bunker. We recognized Bormann, Stumpfegger and Kempka. We didn't run to join them because it looked so dangerous and you could hear machine guns and bullets crackling in the street. We thought we would let them go first and then maybe go over later if things quietened. And then the next moment, as we were talking about this, the tank blew up. It must have been hit by a shell or something because there was a sudden flash from where the turret joined the body and then an instant of shimmering blackness all around it as if the air was shaking. It lurched and stopped and there were flames coming out of it. I didn't see any soldiers get out. Nor did I see what happened to Stumpfegger but I did see Bormann blown over on to his back with his hands in the air just as if he was on stage, acting being blown up. We felt the blast where we were standing, a wall of air that took your breath away as if someone had punched you in the stomach. You must have felt it too. Kempka was rolling on the ground behind the tank but I saw him get up and run away. I never saw Bormann or Stumpfegger again and thought they must be dead. I didn't feel a sliver of sorrow for either of them. But they were not dead, I think.'

He sipped his brandy. 'They both died but later, though still near the bridge. Probably suicide when they realized they couldn't get across. Their bodies weren't discovered until quite recently. Kempka survived and reached the

Americans. I interviewed him before he died. He was convinced that Bormann must have been killed then but I suspect he was only knocked out.'

'Is that what you are doing with me, Hans – interviewing?'

He smiled. 'You have an outstanding memory, Edith. Better – more sequential – than the others.'

'Would you like me to go on?'

'Please.'

Again she looked at him and again there was no indication of anything other than detached impersonal curiosity. Was it possible that he could have expunged it from his own memory, an extreme instance of the suppression he so disapproved of? Was it possible that he had interpreted what had happened quite, quite differently? What was not possible was that she was wrong.

'Do you really want me to continue, Hans?'

'Of course, why not?'

'Very well.'

She sipped her own brandy. She had never really liked it and didn't now, but it was good to have something to hand.

'We left that place, the bridge and the tank, and wandered, I don't know where. You were always a little behind us, so as not to get us into trouble, you said, but to be ready to help us out if we fell into it. I remember Constanze Manziarly asking if you were coming with us all the way to the British or Americans, and you said you probably would. You had your gun.

'Eventually we came to a large junction of four or five roads and tramlines, with two trams stuck in the middle and lots of people. We crossed it to a small square on the other side with apartments and a garage, also a water stand-pipe. Most of the buildings in the square had been bombed and there was no one else there. It seemed quieter and safer than the junction with the trams. We drank and rested and discussed what to do. You kept to the side of the square with your gun. Gerda and the two Chancellery secretaries decided to go and explore, to see if there was a safer way ahead. They would come back and tell us. Traudl would wait by the water pipe while Constanze and I went into the tenements to see if we could find any women's jackets. Those jackets again, you see, that absurd obsession with useless jackets. You were going to stay where you were.

'But you didn't. You followed us into one of the buildings, a set of apartments. Everything was so wrecked inside we couldn't get up the staircase. The ceilings had come down and there was plaster and beams and broken furniture every-where, and a horrible smell. It looked as if it might fall down at any moment. We left it and headed for another set of apartments next to the garage. There was a kind of tunnel entrance next to the garage leading, I think, through an archway to the workshop. The entrance to these other apartments looked in better condition and so I went in, but Constanze didn't. She said she would try the next one, to save time. I went in alone. We never saw Constanze again.'

Edith paused, to see what he would say. At first he said nothing and then, quietly, 'And then?'

It had become a trial of strength. She no longer asked herself why; there would be time for that later. She swallowed and continued.

'I entered into the tenement building. It was cool inside and not as badly damaged as the other. There was a standard lamp upturned in the hall and a red curtain lying on the floor and lots of broken glass, of course. But that was nothing. There was broken glass everywhere you went in Berlin. It was almost cold in there, and quite dark, even though it was still daylight outside. I felt sure it was empty, utterly empty. It had that feel about it, a complete absence of anything human, just things. I was not frightened.

'I opened the first door I came to, which was the apartment on the right. There was a dark little hall and a smell I couldn't place but didn't like, not a strong smell but not a nice one. I wondered at first if it was the gas but it wasn't like gas. I thought perhaps it came from the lavatory but it wasn't quite like that, either. Anyway, I decided I would not take any jacket from that apartment, even if I found one, in case that should smell too. But I went on out of curiosity. To the right the hall gave on to a large dining room facing the square. It was a high-ceilinged room, typical of the turn of the century, with heavy dark wallpaper and a thick dark carpet. There was a black dining table with matching chairs – ten or twelve of them – arranged along the table but pulled well back from it. On the table was a body.

'It was an old woman. I say old – she was probably in her late fifties or early sixties – but that seemed old to us, then. She had bare feet and wore a long light-blue cotton dressing gown. Someone had placed her matching blue slippers neatly on the floor at the foot of the table. They reminded me of Eva's shoes in the bunker when she died, placed just as carefully. The dressing gown was belted at her waist and her hands were folded neatly on her breast. They were greyish-white, her hands, and very thin with prominent veins. Her dressing gown was pulled up around her throat. Whoever had put her there had taken some trouble but there was no cushion beneath her head so it was tilted right back on the table, with her mouth wide open. She had grey hair tinted blonde which spread on the table beneath her instead of being tidied. Perhaps whoever it was had had to leave in a hurry. One of the chairs by the head of the table was on its side. Her eyes were open – they were grey-blue – and the skin of her face looked like parchment that would crumble if you touched it.

'I stood looking at her – it – for some time. Before we left the bunker I had never in my life seen a dead body. Then I

169

had seen scores, hundreds, but this was the first I had looked at. I wondered about her – what her name was, how her life had been, whether she had married. There were no rings but they might have been taken off. And whether there were children, grandchildren, how she had died. Also, who had laid her out with such care, and then abandoned her hurriedly. How her voice sounded. It was strange to me because it was the first time I had felt the absence that is death. Whatever life is, it was not there. The body is not it. The smell was worse in that room.

'And then you came in. You had followed me. And you looked at the body and then at me, and said, "Well, Edith." You said it very meaningfully, as if we were both about to decide something.'

Hans's white shirt front rose and fell with his breathing but his shadowed face was immobile.

THIRTEEN

'I used to wonder what you were thinking,' Edith continued. 'Of course, I know what was on your mind but what were your actual thought processes? Was there a rationale? Did you think to yourself, "I am alone with her. There may never be another time. We ourselves may perish soon"? Or did you think, "She is more vulnerable, less likely to resist, in the presence of death. Death can be erotic, after all. Not directly but by way of contrast. One experiences a sudden need to assert life, to make the most of being amongst the quick and not yet the dead. A biological reaction, perhaps. Continue the species." Is that how you thought, or did you not think at all, but simply do it?'

He said nothing.

Did he want every sordid detail, described by her as part of his personal pornography of the past? Almost literal pornography, in this case. Would he then quibble about definitions and details? In fact, she could not recall every last detail. Remembering the past was like remembering a dream; you might be completing parts of the picture in the act of describing them. But she didn't need to remember every detail.

Angered by his reaction, she forced herself to her feet once more and put another log on the fire, poking it energetically. Now that she had the poker, she could kill him with it, she thought. Better that than the other way round, but even less likely. She could wave it at him, threaten him, make it look as if she was going to, just to frighten him. He deserved something. She laid the poker back in the hearth.

'It wasn't only me, was it?' he said. 'It took two of us.'

'Hardly.' She sat and breathed deeply a couple of times, to control herself. 'Perhaps you were not shocked by what we had found. I was and I accepted your – your comfort, as I at first interpreted it. I didn't accept what developed. I was not fully consulted, you might say.' She remembered the feel of the thick carpet as she lay on it, his weight upon her. When she turned her head – to the right, she remembered the feel of the fibres against her cheek – she was facing the dead woman's slim blue slippers, side on, very close. She could see the underside of the table, too, and at the far end a strand of the woman's grey hair hanging down. And he would not stop, despite her protests. She remembered thinking how willingly, under other circumstances, she might have given him what he was now taking.

'Tell me exactly what you remember of it,' she said. 'How you felt. How you thought I felt, that sort of thing. Did you think I wanted it really, that I didn't mean no?'

'Almost certainly I remember less of it than you,' he said, quietly now. 'I think I thought you didn't really mind.'

That was candour, of a sort; an implied admission. Was that what she wanted, she asked herself – that he should say sorry, I know you didn't want to, I shouldn't have done it, that's what I came to say, why I had to see you now? It was after all what might nowadays be called rape, but not then. It would have been considered her fault for letting him go too far. Perhaps it was her fault, if it were a fault to be weak, tired, shocked, afraid. He had taken advantage of her, that was all; nature's prompting perhaps, just as nature prompted women to bear and rear children. But that was only half of it; what would he say about the other thing he had done? He knew that she, and no one else, knew. He would assume she had stayed silent until now only because she had thought him dead. Was he here to make sure she remained silent?

For herself, if she wanted an apology, or even an admission, she would be the living contradiction of everything she had said about the past. It would confirm that it did matter, after all, that there was a point in going back. Her demand would vindicate everything he had said about the need to understand, to reconcile it within ourselves, to make sense of ourselves. She was not sure she could bear his pointing that out. But she did want something.

'What then?' he asked in barely more than a whisper. 'What do you remember next?'

He knew what next. She took a deep breath. 'I left the building first, as you may recall. I think you offered to go and look for a jacket for me but I couldn't bear to stay there any longer. Outside in the square I saw Russian soldiers around the stand-pipe, about half a dozen of them. They were clowning about and some were staggering in an exaggerated way, as if acting drunk. But they were drunk. They had crates of champagne from somewhere and were swigging from the bottles, then throwing them up in the air to smash when they were empty. More broken glass. Sitting on the ground, just where they were throwing the bottles, were three prisoners. They weren't tied up, they were just sitting there bare headed and covering their faces with their arms whenever the bottles smashed nearby. They were German, of course, I could see from their uniforms, but they didn't look quite right, there was something different about them. I remember feeling relieved that Traudl wasn't still there. She must have gone away, thinking we weren't coming back. Or escaped.

'It was too late for me, of course. The soldiers saw me.

They waved and laughed and two who could still walk normally came over. Their manner was not threatening, they were laughing and one of them was holding out a bottle for me. I didn't know where to go. They came up to me and said things in Russian I didn't understand. Then I remembered what we had been told – cigarettes, give them cigarettes. I had some in the pockets of the army jacket I was supposed to have got rid of. I gave them a packet and they thanked me, bowing, and lit them straight away. They tried to get me to drink but I pushed the bottle away and shook my head. They were no more than boys, really, younger than me. One was short with a round red face and smooth skin. In other circumstances, a kindly face, you could imagine his mother's in it, an anxious peasant woman in a headscarf. He smiled all the time. The other was tall and pale, with bad acne and his front teeth missing. He nodded a lot, with his mouth open. It made him seem stupid, but perhaps he was simply shy, I thought then.

They led me towards the others, fingering my army jacket and asking about it. I could guess what they were asking, of course, but I just shrugged and smiled and shook my head. I was frightened and trying not to show it. Then they stopped and the short one repeated, "Papers, papers," in German. We were closer to the others then and I could see the prisoners more clearly. They were those same three boys, the Hitler Youth we had seen waiting for tanks in the hole in the road. Only now they didn't look at all dangerous or fanatical. They were just frightened little boys staring at me. They must've hoped I could help them. But the Russian soldier kept poking me and repeating, "Papers, papers." I couldn't do anything about the boys. I couldn't do anything.'

She sipped her brandy, this time without noticing the taste. 'While I was trying to get my Chancellery identity card out of my pocket they took me by the arms and started marching me away towards that dark tunnel next to the garage. They were still smiling and laughing. One of the others by the water pump called out something and then everyone laughed. I laughed, too, to try to make it seem as if I was one of them and not frightened, but I was terrified. I was still trying to get my card out as we approached the tunnel but they kept hold of my upper arm and seemed to have lost interest in who I was. Then, just before the tunnel, I looked back and saw you.'

She looked at him now. He remained utterly still, with the stillness of rapture. Shame, embarrassment, fear, apology, regret, denial, anger or any other emotion she might have expected, but not this childlike absorption. His eyes were bright. She hated him at that moment, wanting to make him suffer. They stared at each other for some seconds more, before she continued as slowly and precisely as she could force herself to be.

'You were standing in the entrance to the building we had been in, looking towards me. You had your gun, none of the soldiers had seen you. I called out to you, "My papers, they say they want my papers, but they are taking me into the tunnel." The soldiers who held me looked round and saw you but they just carried on, they didn't seem worried or even interested in you, even though you could have shot them. Perhaps they were too drunk to care. You could have shot them.' She paused and sipped again. 'We were almost in the tunnel and I started struggling, trying to hang back, but they forced me forward. I screamed out to you again, "Hans, the tunnel, they are taking me into the tunnel!" But you did nothing. You watched them drag me into it. You just stood there, with your gun.'

She stopped and waited. The silence lengthened, she had no idea for how long. Eventually, he said quietly, 'What then?'

'Have you read an English novel by a Polish writer – *Lord Jim*, by Joseph Conrad?'

'A Pole?' He shook his head.

'In it, a man on a sinking ship loses his nerve at the moment of crisis. He has been brave and honourable until that moment, but this time, suddenly, for the only time in his life, he is a coward. No one knows this at the time or afterwards, except him, but it haunts him for the rest of his life. You saw what they were doing with me that afternoon,

177

Hans. You knew what they intended to do, yet you stood and watched. You had your gun and you did nothing. Except, except what you then did.'

She felt she was going to cry. It was absurd, after all these years, absurd and humiliating. It made her angry with herself. She could not bear the thought of humiliating herself in front of him. But it was rising in her like nausea and had almost broken through her voice as she said, 'And you did nothing.' She gulped some brandy, waited, then spoke again, carefully.

'Was this episode your Lord Jim moment, Hans? Is that why you cannot leave it alone?'

His eyes were still staring but the rest of his face was sunken and drained of hue, like a cadaver's. A pornographer sated, she thought. 'Was that it?' she persisted. 'Is that what it was for you?'

'Go on.' His voice was faint, his breathing was becoming laboured.

'Somehow I broke away from them and ran towards you. I was shouting at you – "Hans, help me!" – something like that. The two soldiers were running after me. I was aware that some of the other soldiers were running too, but whether after me or not I didn't know. It was like a speeded-up dream and it's hard to remember the sequence now. Someone fired a gun, more than once, or more than one gun. As I got nearer you I could see you weren't looking at me. You put down your gun and raised your hands above your head, facing the soldiers, ignoring me. I never reached you, as you know. I fell and they caught up with me, or they caught me and I fell. Anyway, they had me by the arms again and dragged me away. I was crying and calling out to you.'

'Did you see what happened next?' His voice was still faint.

'Not immediately next. I was being dragged across the square towards the tunnel. But before they got me in I saw what you did.' She nodded, her eyes on his. 'Yes, Hans, I saw what you did.'

He was by the stand-pipe with the other soldiers. The three boy prisoners were still seated, looking on in fearful fascination as their drunken captors gesticulated and shouted at each other. They had given Hans a bottle and watched him drain it, champagne running from his mouth. As soon as he finished he hurled the bottle high into the air. The soldiers cheered as it smashed, harmlessly far away. There was more gesticulating with this time some pointing at the prisoners. Then one of the soldiers gave Hans his gun back. Hans stepped aside and in one swift movement cocked it and raised it to his shoulder, pointing it at the prisoners. The soldier who had given it to him swayed and smiled. The three young prisoners gazed up at him, then crumpled like puppets at the abrupt clatter of automatic fire.

'I saw it,' she repeated.

He cleared his throat and looked again at his brandy glass, which he was holding at a dangerous angle. 'I suppose that might now be called a war crime.'

'What are called war crimes are war crimes.'

'A category that did not then exist.' He spoke with sudden energy. 'It was war, that's what it was. Just war. What war has always been. Those boys were about to be shot anyway. The Russians hated and despised the Hitler Youth. They weren't going to let them become prisoners. It began with me pleading on their behalf. Really, it did. One of the Russians, the one who handed me my weapon, had a little German. He said the only way for the boys to avoid being shot by them was if I did it. If I didn't, he would do it immediately, only he would shoot them in the stomach so that they would most likely die slowly, in agony. What would you have done, Edith? What would anyone have done?' His manner was almost truculent now.

'I would not have shot them. I could not have done it. Your own side, your own people. Children.'

'They were going to kill them, I tell you, they would have been dead within minutes anyway. The alternative for those boys was not immortality, or old age, or even maturity. It was the same thing, a few minutes later.'

'You could have turned your gun on the Russians.'

He raised one hand and let it fall. 'They kept their word, I kept mine.'

'So it was a deal? Your freedom for their lives?'

He leaned forward, his face now out of the shadow, lined and hard. 'All life was a deal then, not only after Berlin fell but before, all through the Nazi period. You did the deal and survived if you were lucky, or you didn't. The deal I did then was just a dramatized version of what we all did in Berlin at that time. Life was compromises or trade-offs, every day, one after another, big or small, life and death or cigarettes for food, it came to the same thing. And those who sit in judgement on us now, in comfortable chairs in air-conditioned rooms, and afterwards drive home to talk about it in nice safe houses over good dinners and wine with friends – these people have no right to judge what we did in circumstances they have no idea of, no idea at all. No one should judge themselves or others for what they did then. If there is to be judgement, the only people with a right to judge are those who were there.'

'I was there. I do judge you.'

He smiled with patent insincerity. 'And what is your judgement, Edith?'

'What do you think?'

He kept his grin, now a mere baring of teeth. 'That I am a cold-blooded killer, I suppose.'

'A murderer. You murdered your own to save your own skin.'

He leaned back in his chair again. His face was once more

181

in shadow though his white shirt front appeared to quiver for a few seconds as if her words had pinned him, twitching, to the back of the chair. It pleased her to have such an effect.

'Things were different then,' he said eventually. 'A different world.'

She made herself smile. 'So the past is another country after all?'

He leaned forward once more, determinedly. 'Whatever we say about the past, only you and I know this, Edith. We can forget the Russian soldiers. They never knew who I was. They let me go with my weapon. They couldn't be bothered with me. They were drunk and now they're almost certainly dead. So you and I are the only living people who know. You and I, Edith.' He paused. 'What happened to you afterwards?'

She looked at her empty glass. The triumph of hitting home made her more inclined to be expansive, but she still had to steel herself to tell it. She wished her glass were not empty. 'They dragged me into the tunnel. It was dark, with an earth floor covered with rubble. I kept stumbling and trying to hang back. They pushed me up against the wall. My head banged against it and they started tugging at my jacket. That was when I pulled off my earrings to offer them. I was doing anything I could think of to distract or delay them. They were not very rough with me, they didn't hit me, they just kept pushing me and pulling at my clothes. I don't think they really knew what to do. I was crying and shaking my head and saying, "Please stop, please stop, you can have everything, leave me, please." But they just kept on. I could still do things, I was still on my feet, but I couldn't stop them doing what they were doing. It was like a dream. Then when they knocked my hand and one of my earrings fell to the ground I cried out and pointed to where it had gone. That distracted them and, believe it or not, they stopped and bent down to look. For a moment. That was when I could have run but my legs refused to move. Then I had my idea.

'I grinned and mimed frantically, like an idiot. I pointed to each of them, then to myself, then put my hands together against one side of my face as if it were a pillow, then pointed back out of the tunnel, then pointed at the dirty ground and made a face and shook my head. Finally I offered them my arms to take me, as when they had dragged me in. I know where there is a bed, I was miming. I will willingly go with you there, but not here, on the dirty ground. They understood, spoke to each other, nodded, and led me out by the arms. They were simple boys, peasant boys, so young. And not unpleasant, not really. That was the awful thing.

'Of course, my idea was very vague. It was just to get us out of the tunnel to where there were other people, even if they were other soldiers. I didn't know what would happen then. As soon as we got out I looked to see if you were there but you weren't, of course. You'd made your escape.

The Russian soldiers were still there, drinking and arguing, and the three boys lay where you'd shot them. Then I had the idea of leading my two back into the apartment where you and I had been, in case you were hiding inside. It was very unlikely, I know, but I desperately hoped you were. I still hoped you might protect me, you see. After all, if you were willing to use your gun, then perhaps I could escape. Even if they killed you I might still escape. That's how desperate I was.

'I indicated the entrance and they took me to it. When we got into the hall I called out for you. They didn't understand that and told me to shut up. Then one of them pushed open the door to the apartment we had been in. They were looking for a room with a bed, I suppose, which gave me my next idea. I nodded to the right and they took me into the dining room where that woman was laid out upon the table. I was so relieved she was still there. Not that anyone was likely to have moved her. They stopped when they saw her. They were shocked. They let go of my arms. I pointed to the body and to me and went and kissed it on the forehead. It was stone cold and it smelt worse, close up. I was pretending it was my mother.

'And do you know what they did, those boys? They stared at her, took off their army caps, crossed themselves and knelt down and prayed. Seconds before they were going to rape me, now they were praying for me and for the soul of my mother, kneeling on the carpet where we had been. They were more respectful of death than you had been, Hans.

'Then they went. They just left. I was standing by the body with my hand on her cold forehead, and they got to their feet, still clutching their caps in both hands. They bowed to me, crossed themselves again, and went. I stayed. I was shaking too much to move. I stayed a long time. For years afterwards, almost every day, I used to wonder who she was. I wished I could have thanked her.'

He picked at the spot of food on his shirt. 'You should pray for her.'

'If I prayed I would.'

'You are lady of the manor here, next to the church, but you don't go to it?'

'Oh yes, I go to church. Regularly. But I don't pray, not really.'

'We should all pray, even if we do not believe. It is good for us.'

'You find it good, Hans?'

He looked at her, clearly and solemnly now. 'Yes, I do.'

'What do you pray about?'

'For forgiveness.'

'I suppose that's the point.' It was some sort of acknowledgement, perhaps. She felt very tired again. 'Well, I think we've done it all, don't you? Trawled it all up, all the

185

ALAN JUDD

unwanted and irredeemable. There can't be anything else. It's time for bed.'

'You don't want to know what happened to me, Edith?'

She got carefully to her feet. 'No, Hans, I don't.'

'I can understand that.'

It was an irritating reply. She said nothing.

'May we take a walk before bed?' he asked.

'Another walk?'

'I like to walk around the garden before bed. It settles the mind, helps one sleep. Even if you cannot see the garden and even if it is raining. Sometimes, especially if it is raining. It soothes one.'

'You can if you want. You can use the same waterproofs and boots.'

'You will not accompany me?'

'My knees are bad tonight. Also, I can't be bothered to put on boots and things.' In fact, a little gentle use would probably benefit her knees; she had been sitting for too long. Nor was the idea of a slow perambulation on the wet grass in the gentle rain – only just audible now – as unappealing as she had first thought it. 'But you can go if you like.'

'Please, Edith, it would be nice together. We could finish our conversation.'

'I thought we had.'

He remained seated, looking at her. She would have to show him to the scullery, then make sure he had the right

186

things. It was almost as much trouble as going herself. 'Very well, then. Not for long.'

He got up slowly, smiling despite the effort, 'That sounds like Edith of old.'

'I don't think so.'

FOURTEEN

The scullery bulb had gone. 'You can do something useful for me. You are tall enough to reach it with a chair from the kitchen. There should be a new bulb in the dresser drawer.'

The effort of stretching and replacing the bulb made him wheeze. 'My asthma,' he repeated. 'I never used to have it. I have to take a spray everywhere with me because it could be fatal. It affects my heart. I have a weak heart.'

She found an old cape for him, marked with a faded War Department arrow and, in thick black lettering, Cape Monsoon Rain. A shiny black sou'wester, covered in cobwebs, and Michael's Wellingtons completed his rain-proofing. She put on her galoshes, her gardening coat and her ancient broad-brimmed tweed hat. She looked a sight, she knew – an eccentric old bag, Michael had called her – but there was no one to see her. She didn't count Hans.

Rain must have swollen the door because the bolts were too stiff for her to move and she had to ask him to undo them. As he did so she noticed that he had in one hand the heavy iron scraper she kept by the Aga, a relic of the previous solid fuel oven. This oil-fired successor did not need it but for twenty years the scraper had nonetheless remained in its old place, on the floor at the side.

'What've you got that for?' she asked.

'This?' He held it up and looked at it, as if he had forgotten about it and was surprised to find it in his hand. 'Well, we are going outside, into the dark. It is sometimes good to carry a weapon, just in case. You never know. I am not the young man I was, I couldn't fight someone off with only my hands.'

This was as bad as the poker, worse because there was less reason. But she didn't want to show her fear and disbelief and so tried to sound briskly dismissive. 'Don't be ridiculous. No one's going to be waiting on the lawn in the pouring rain to attack us. We're more likely to be attacked in town or in our beds. How is anyone to know we're out for a walk on a night like this? They'd think we were mad.'

He smiled. 'Perhaps I should take it to bed too, then.'

'We've never been burgled here.'

He shrugged but made no move to put it back. She wanted to demand that he did but she could feel herself trembling slightly and worried that her voice would betray her. She told herself she was being ridiculous, that of course he didn't want to murder her. On the other hand she and she alone knew what he had done already, and why else carry an iron scraper?

They left the door open so they could see their way up the wet brick steps and on to the lawn. The rain was less gentle than it sounded from within and the dark lawn squelched beneath their feet. The insistent tapping on her protected head and shoulders might have been soothing under different circumstances, as Hans had said. She longed to be alone, and warm and dry in her bed.

It was densely dark. She sensed rather than saw that they were nearing the beech hedge at the side. It was no good trying to lose him. They were too close to the house and he would find his way back. 'We should head more into the middle,' she said. 'Veer left.'

He put his arm through hers. 'I am in your hands, Edith. It is pleasant, this rain, isn't it? A beautiful sound. Just listen to it. I told you. Also, it is very relaxing to talk without seeing each other, don't you think?'

If his eyesight was poor it might offer some hope if it came to a chase, though she couldn't imagine being able to run now. She concentrated on avoiding the rose beds, guiding them outwards towards the ha-ha. Miles beyond that, across drenched rolling fields, dripping woods and a small marsh to the side of the Downs, was the sea. In clear weather you could always see it from the lawn, a fine thin horizon – silver, blue or grey – but you could never see it in the rain. You could, however, smell it. She could smell it now. She went on about it at unnecessary length. Still clutching the implement in his fist, he patted her hand with his knuckles.

'It must be very beautiful. Things have turned out very well for you, Edith.'

'What did you do afterwards?' she asked, 'after I was taken away? You were captured, you said?'

'Yes, not then but later, quite a bit later. I crossed the square back the way we had come to the large junction with the two trams you described. There weren't so many people then and I looked around for the rest of the party but couldn't see them. I will confess to you now what I have not told anyone before: I felt bad for not trying to save you. I still do.'

'But not so bad as to do anything about it.'

'No. To my shame.' Their boots squelched on the sodden grass. 'I even looked in the trams for the others. One had been hit by a shell and was a wreck, with bodies in it, but the other was untouched and empty. It must have stopped because its way was blocked. I suddenly felt very tired, exhausted, and so I climbed to the upper deck and went to sleep on the floor. I slept until after dark.'

'You were lucky.'

'We were both lucky. We survived.' They stopped at the ha-ha. 'I am sorry if I alarm you, Edith.'

'Alarm me?'

He held up the implement again. 'By carrying this. You are doubtless right that it is not necessary. I see that now. I am not used to the country, you see, and really I was think-ing that animals – those cows with horns – might attack us. You probably think I am mad, but I am not mad. At least, not in the sense we were discussing. Just silly.' He paused briefly, then continued before she could think what to say. 'Now I must ask you a difficult question, one you may quite understandably find upsetting. But it is necessary to ask it. My question is this: have you told the full story of the Russian soldiers? Are you quite sure you have left nothing out?'

She could not prevent her hand tightening on his arm, gripping it through the wet cape.

He patted her hand again with his knuckles. 'It is all right, Edith. Your silence is eloquent.'

She removed her hand, not trusting herself to speak. His tone was condescending, almost gloating. She was upset, angry and still frightened, but determined not to let him triumph, as he would see it. After a deep breath and with a carefully levelled voice, she said, 'It is true that one of them got me on to the ground in the tunnel, the shorter one, the one with the kind face. It was after that, after' –

she swallowed – 'after he got off, that I distracted them with my earring and persuaded them to come to the apartment. They must have thought they would have a more comfortable time. When we got there it happened as I described.'

The wind got up again, blowing the rain into their faces, straight off the distant sea. She was glad of it.

'Thank you, Edith, you have pleased me greatly. Now we are equal. We each know something – something important – about the other.'

She stood with clenched teeth, staring into the billowing darkness, tears mingling with the rain on her face. She wanted to sob, to cry aloud, to throw herself down, to push him away, to grab the iron claw and kill him. But she was determined not to give him the satisfaction he sought. She remained silent, her determination growing harder and colder.

'Many young women in Germany at that time must have found themselves in your position,' he continued. 'There is nothing to be ashamed of. Like my own so-called war crime, it was commoner than we think. How curious that the past should have put us both in the same position now, each with something we do not want examined. The past is not another country after all, it is here and now. Very much so, don't you think?'

He spoke quietly, looking down at her. His relish was

almost palpable, like a lecherous intent. She clenched her fists in her pockets, controlled her breathing and continued to face straight into the wind and rain.

'What do you want?' she wanted to shout, but instead she spoke with deliberate mildness. 'What puzzles me most is you, Hans.'

'I?' he laughed, a little too heartily. 'What puzzles you about me? You know everything important about me already, I think.'

'Is it that you simply wanted to confess what you did? Is that why you wanted to see me?'

'I have nothing to confess. What I did was not a crime. It was a mercy killing. It is only people who have never been in such circumstances who see differently.'

'Or is it that you wanted – she hesitated – 'to make sure that I was not going to reveal it?'

'As I told you, my interest is in exploring the past. That is all.'

'Other people's pasts?'

'They constitute one's own.' He put his arm around her shoulders with a gentleness that contrasted with his tone. 'It is so nice that after all this time we have so much in common, so much to share.'

She hoped he didn't feel her shudder. She turned back towards the house, slowly, so as not to alert him to her fear.

They walked in step towards the homely lights, the rain

on their backs now. 'So are we really the last two alive, of all who were in the bunker?' she asked.

'I think so. In the Führerbunker, anyway. There might be people who visited but none who was based there, so far as I know. During the past twenty years I have seen nearly everyone who survived.'

'And now they are all dead?'

'Except us.'

'Killed by you?' she wanted to ask. 'In case they knew from me what you had done? Did you track them all down over the years, get them to talk about it and then discreetly murder them?' But if that were true it would have made more sense to start with her, not finish.

'Quite a few of us' – she had to make herself refer to them as 'us' – 'survived to a good age.'

'Yes, it is surprising, especially those of us who were in the Russian camps. If you got out alive and survived the few years afterwards – not all did – there seems to have been no effect on longevity. We were a surprisingly robust group. Hitler would no doubt have attributed it to his master-race theory.'

'He would need to compare it with the survival rates of concentration camp victims. They were presumably not master race.'

'A good point.'

As they took off their dripping hats, coats and boots in the scullery, she surreptitiously studied his face. It had misled her before, in 1945, when he had turned out not to be the man she thought, so there could be no reading it now. Although lined and drawn, like parchment, it was still a benign face, that of a patient, elderly man. Perhaps he would murder benignly, saying 'You must understand, Edith, that there is nothing personal in this. I am very fond of you, as I have always been. It is just that, as before when the Russians took you, and as with those three boys, I have no choice. I am sure you will understand.'

He put the iron claw on the floor as he bent to take off his boots. It was not easy for him and she was quicker at taking off her galoshes. While he was busy with his boots she picked up the claw and took it into the kitchen, pushing it into the narrow gap between the Aga and the wall, out of sight. He straightened as she returned to the scullery, staring at her. She couldn't tell whether he had forgotten it or had seen her take it. Keep him talking, she thought.

'How about a nightcap? Brandy, whisky?'

He shook his head. 'Thank you, Edith. It is late and I have had enough. It is time for bed. Whether or not we sleep much at our age is another matter, of course, but it is time to try. You have been most hospitable to me, most kind. One last request: please show me to my room. I am not sure I could find it again in such a large house.'

She led him upstairs, habitually switching off the lights as they went. She regretted it; she would have felt safer with them on. 'I always leave the landing light on,' she pretended when they reached the top of the stairs. 'Yours is the principal guest room along the corridor on the right.' The stairs had left him breathing heavily and wheezing again, which was reassuring. He would not be able to chase her, provided she could run.

'And yours?' he asked as his breathing recovered. 'Which is your room?'

She gestured vaguely. 'Along there.' She offered him her hand to shake, so that there could be no ambiguity. 'Good night, Hans.'

Instead of shaking her hand, he took it and kissed it, bowing and clicking his heels with rusty formality. 'I cannot thank you enough, Edith. Our conversation has been both a revelation and a lesson to me. It means a great deal to me that we have met again.'

She made herself smile.

Once in her room, with the door firmly closed, she remained standing by the dressing table, holding on to it. Her legs trembled and she wanted badly to sit or lie down but she feared she might not be able to get up again in a hurry. She must think, she told herself. Not feel, think. As when she was with those two Russians, keep thinking no matter what. It worked then, more or less.

There was no lock on her bedroom door. She could put a

piece of furniture against it, as they did in films, and with luck he would be too weak to move it. But she was too weak to put it there. She could creep downstairs to the telephone and ring the police. He probably would not hear her. For the first time in her life she wished she had a mobile telephone. But it would be hard to explain to the police and he might deny it all and they might believe him and think she was just a batty old bag. Seeing herself in the dressing-table mirror – haggard, her eyes reddened, her hair awry, one earring missing, a hole in her tights and a stain, she noticed with irritation, on the breast of her dress – she could not blame them.

After a while she had an idea; it did pay to think, it always did. She gathered her nightdress, her dressing gown and her slippers and quietly opened the door. There was no sign of him. The only sounds were the wind and the ticking of the hall clock. The landing light did not illuminate his end of the corridor but she could see that his door was closed, with his light showing beneath it. Switching off her own bedroom light and closing the door as soundlessly as she could, she crept farther along the corridor to the end room that had been Michael's when he was a boy and now served for visiting grandchildren. Neither of the beds was aired, of course, but that didn't matter; anyway, she doubted she would sleep.

Once there she sat on the end of the child's single bed, reluctant to undress. But as time passed and there were no sounds, she began to feel cold and ridiculous. She changed into her nightclothes, crept into the bathroom across the corridor, then went to bed.

But not to sleep. Her body was weary but her mind was filled with anxiety, fear and curiosity. It had been naïve of her to co-operate with his excavation of her past. What had at first seemed a harmless if pointless passion had become something altogether more sinister and unsettling. Provided nothing happened her anxiety would die away, she knew, smothered by the daily accretions of her quiet domestic life. Even her memories of the Russian boys might lie still again, despite their recent exhumation. She could at least hope for that. But for now the spectres and fears he raised twisted and turned in the guts of her mind, leaving her writhing in guilt beyond reason, fear without end. As to his own crime, what was he trying to do – expiate it or bury it? If the latter, would it entail burying her?

The knocking made her limbs jerk and she almost cried out. She must have been dozing after all. She lay with her eyes open wide in the dark, her blood pounding in her ears, her flesh prickling, her muscles tense but paralysed. She could not move, she knew she could not move, even if he came in now. She listened, every nerve straining in the silence. Perhaps she had imagined or dreamt it.

It came again, three knocks, soft but definite, yet definitely not on this door. He must be knocking at her own door.

That he should have bothered to knock was perhaps a good sign. Did murderers bother to knock?

'Edith? Edith?' he called quietly.

She lay unanswering. Faintly, she heard his footsteps shuffling back along the corridor. It sounded as if he were wearing slippers, perhaps also a good sign. Maybe he genuinely wanted something, had forgotten where his bathroom was, something like that. Her limbs obeyed her now. She got slowly out of bed by turning on her side and half rolling out – there was no other way these days – then tiptoed to the door and opened it. The handle made a noise but the door did not squeak on its hinges. Peering round, she saw the old man shuffling back across the landing. He was wearing a faded yellow dressing gown and appeared to drag one foot slightly. His white hair was tousled, exposing the bald patch on the back of his head. He looked reassuringly vulnerable. He returned to his room and closed the door.

These were not the actions of a would-be murderer, she thought. They were the actions of an old man wanting something. But what? She speculated fruitlessly for a few more minutes, then put on her own dressing gown and slippers and followed him. Whatever it was that he might want, there was still something that she wanted. She paused at his door, listening. The bedside light was still on, there was some sort of movement, the sound of bed springs and a sigh or exhalation.

She knocked. 'Hans?'

'Come in.'

He was sitting up in bed with a notebook open before him and a pencil in his hand. He wore his glasses and blue and white striped pyjamas. His white eyebrows looked bushier. 'Edith, I have just been along to your room but I thought you must be asleep. I was surprised because I heard a lavatory flush a short while before so I concluded you were awake.'

'I heard you call but I was only half awake and wasn't sure whether I was dreaming,' she said. 'What did you want?'

He closed his notebook and smiled. 'To continue our conversation, that is all. There is so much that is interesting. My mind is full of it and I couldn't sleep. When I heard the lavatory I thought perhaps it was the same for you.'

'Have you been making notes of what I was saying?'

'Yes. I always do. I have made notes of everything that all the others have told me. I have many volumes of these notebooks, an archive almost. I believe I must be the best-informed person alive on what actually happened in and after the bunker.'

He had folded his clothes on the only chair in the room. She wanted neither to touch them nor to give him an excuse to get out of bed. She eased herself carefully on to the very edge of his mattress at the foot of the bed. 'Are you writing a book?'

'A book? Me?' He smiled and shook his head.

'Then why, Hans, why? I still don't fully understand.'

'I have told you why. Because it is important for every human being to come to terms with his or her past. It is particularly important for we Germans to come to terms with ours, neither ignoring it, nor glorying in it, nor wallowing in the guilt it bequeaths us. And because it is even more important for us, we, who were closest to the flame that tried to consume the world and ended by consuming itself, we who acted in the final drama, to come to terms with what happened to us, with what we did, were and are.'

He was like an evangelist, she thought, his aged face illumined from within by the fervour of passionate conviction. She had seen it in religious people of all denominations, in political enthusiasts of all persuasions, in campaigners for manifold causes, in youthful Nazis. Genuine believers all, good and bad, passionate and sincere. As if sincerity were ever enough.

'And now I must ask you yet one more question, Edith. A favour, since this is not the only time I have asked a last question. Please would you describe once again your dance with Eva at the end of that drunken party. You have evoked it vividly but I am sure there is more detail to come. You remember: she had been dancing with Fegelein and was clearly enraptured. But she became self-conscious, perhaps when she saw you watching. Another witness told me that she left him and asked you to dance with her.'

He opened his notebook and adjusted his spectacles, like an official going through some routine procedure. Or a methodical pornographer, a meticulous record-keeper. 'Perhaps your natural self-effacement led you to leave out that detail. Please describe it, if you can. I wish to check that I have got it right.'

She looked at him. It was conceivable that his was, at heart, an erotic quest. Almost necrophiliac in this case. 'Yes, I danced with Eva Braun. She came across to me after leaving Fegelein. She was flushed as if she had been dancing energetically, although it was a slow dance, a waltz, I suppose. I can't recall the tune now but it was the one I told you of, over and over again. That being the only record.'

'"Blood-red roses tell you of happiness", was the refrain.' He coughed.

'Eva stood in front of me, looking into my eyes, and said, "Please, Edith, please will you dance with me?" She seemed excited or upset, or both. So we danced together. That is, we shuffled around doing a kind of waltz, a two-step, really. We never sorted out who was supposed to be lead. There was no need, it wasn't necessary, no one led. We went together. Her hands and body were hot, very hot. I could feel the heat of her through her dress. She held me tightly, pressing herself against me. I think she wanted comfort. We didn't speak. Our stomachs and legs pressed against each other. I could feel from her thighs which way she was going. She was a good dancer, Eva. Most of the time she was looking at my shoulder or my neck but sometimes she looked into my eyes. Hers were so sad, and so frightened, and so determined. I wanted to comfort her but there was nothing to say. We just looked into each other's eyes. I felt like crying.'

'How did the dance end?'

'I can't remember. I only remember leaving the party. She was talking to some others then. I remember her saying, "Why do we keep going? Why not just stop? All this killing, it is so pointless."'

'Did she ever say anything about the camps?'

'The concentration camps? Eva? I doubt she gave them a thought.'

Propped up by his pillow, head bent forward, he wrote busily in his notebook. When he lifted his head to speak again he was disrupted by an attack of coughing and wheezing that left him struggling for breath. 'Forgive me,' he said eventually. 'It's my asthma, it comes and goes. There's probably something here I am allergic to.' He paused, wheezing. 'What you have told me is very exciting, Edith. Thank you.'

She waited until his breathing had improved. The attack had made him paler. He was in no position to threaten her.

'But why?' she asked. 'What is your real reason? I don't believe it is just curiosity.'

He stared at her, lips apart, his chest rising and falling beneath his pyjamas.

'Are you afraid of being uncovered as a war criminal?' she continued. 'Do you wish to assure yourself of my silence? Or to silence me? Or is it some sort of control that you seek, control of the past?'

She felt perfectly calm, in control herself now, except that her feet were cold despite her slippers. His face was strained and he looked suddenly older. He stared as if preoccupied with an inner vision, not with her.

'Not for the reasons you think,' he said eventually. 'Not to ensure your silence. I am sure of that anyway. Nor to make money, nor to seek revenge, nor for publicity. I am no threat, Edith, I promise you.'

'Then why?'

'Because I am interested.'

The hall clock struck two. His breathing was more laboured and for a while he could say no more. But when he resumed he spoke with surprising energy and rapidity.

'All right, you say, more than interested. This is most unusual behaviour, to spend twenty years of your life tracking people down, talking to them for no reason other than your own curiosity. It is obsessive, the behaviour of an obsessive, I accept that. You can call it an obsession, if that helps you explain it to yourself. But I am not a dangerous obsessive, I am not a murderer. I am like people who collect stamps or pictures of trains from their childhood, or research their ancestors. But what I collect is different.

'So why this subject? you might ask. Well, I have given you good reasons which satisfied all the others. Curiosity is enough, is it not? Curiosity about what one was oneself involved in? Most people feel that. Of course, the others I talked to did not know what you know, about the three boys. Or about what happened to you. It may sound sur-prising but for me that whole episode, that one hour of our lives, was just a detail, one among many. In these times of concern about war crimes and human rights and other such luxuries of comfortable living, it may seem strange that such events can be mere details but that's what they were, that's how they happened, randomly. As for you, I have no fear that you will say anything, Edith, especially as I have con-firmed that you have your own secret to hide, not a war crime but something very important to you, more important than war crimes, something that lives with you still. One secret guarantees another. I am sure you appreciate that, Edith.

'Anyway, if you wanted to tell the world you would surely have done so by now rather than wait until the late evening of our lives. At the very least you would have wanted to dis-cuss it with the culprit, now that you have him before you, but plainly you did not. I had to drag everything out of you.' He tried to smile but was overtaken by another fit of breathlessness. 'I must take my medicine soon. I could not find it here. It must be in the car. No matter for now. Perhaps you will get it for me in a minute. As for the rest of my war, after we parted, I was lucky: I was wounded right at the end, and taken prisoner by the Russians. Although it took me many years to appreciate that imprisonment, not death, was good luck.

'As years passed after my release I became increasingly interested in the end I had witnessed in part, the end of empire, the fall of the Reich. I wanted to know all, all about all of us, especially the bigwigs, the Golden Pheasants, as they were known.' He patted the mattress beside him. 'Sit by me, why don't you? Come and sit by me.'

She did not move.

'Well, after we parted I was caught up in the last fighting in Berlin, in the thick of it. And it was thick. The air itself thickened, it was acrid, full of fumes and smoke and brick dust so thick you felt the grit on your teeth. Do you remember that? It was never properly light in those last days. I was trying to find a way to cross the river when I fell in with the remnants of an infantry regiment. They were dazed with exhaustion, they'd had weeks of fighting outside the city, ordered, counter-ordered this way and that, ever fewer of them, ever more of the enemy, first under one command, then another, then under a command that never existed at all except in the Führer's imagination. They were heroes, unacknowledged heroes. There were thousands like them. I am not ashamed to say that now.' His eyes seemed remote again, his breathing more laboured. 'I became one of them. The leadership betrayed us soldiers. We fought on when all had abandoned us, when there was no hope, when all the Golden Pheasants had flown. What God abandoned we defended.

'Why, you ask? Because we were German soldiers. That meant something then. We could have won, we should have won if only we had been given the means. If it were not for the Party leadership, those self-seeking fools you and I spent our time with, we would have won. It was pride, the bitter pride of desperation. We preferred annihilation to defeat.' He paused, his eyes on hers again. 'Sit with me, Edith. Why don't you sit with me? You're not afraid that I shall strangle you, are you?'

She looked back at him, unmoving.

'So be it. At the end, the very end, we held the bridge at the western end of the Kurfürstendamm. "We" being I and two ordinary soldiers whose names I never even knew. We were too tired for names, yet for forty-eight hours we held that bridge, armed only with a single machine gun and a stock of Panzerfausts – anti-tank grenades. Quite effective, so long as you were close. The three of us, for two days and two nights, against the might of the Red Army. No one saw it, except our enemies, and most of them were dead. No one gave us medals, no one thanked us, we had nothing to gain, nothing to hope for. We fought on because we were German soldiers, so far as we knew the last German soldiers there would ever be. Until a shell did for us, for my two comrades anyway. I was unconscious and wounded, as I told you. Shells are no respecters of heroism, they don't see it.

'And so, years after, when I was released back into Germany and far enough from it to become curious about what I had been through, I read every account of the bunker I could find. I saw or heard all the interviews. But there is no substitute for talking to those who were there and that is why I started so long ago to do this. Some, of course, were willing to talk to anyone who was interested, Traudl Junge, Gerda Christian, Otto Günsche, others less so. But you were the least willing. You had talked to no one, you'd never tried to make money from your experiences, no one knew where you were or even if you were alive. Now, having found you, I have confirmed what I suspected. I know why. We have much in common, Edith, and I am happy that our secrets are safe with each other. I shall sleep more easily now. Sit by me. Come.'

He raised his hand to pat the mattress again but diverted it to his chest as another coughing fit engulfed him. His last few words were spoken as if he were being strangled. The fit was worse than before and left him gasping, with his hands to his heart.

'Shall I get you some water?' she asked.

He shook his head. 'My asthma treatment from my car,' he breathed. 'If you would be so kind. I cannot move when I am like this. But first let me tell you' – he raised his eyes to hers, panting and staring with a strange, hard glitter – 'let me say that talking to you has been more rewarding for me, and more exciting, than talking to anyone else. Not only because you remember so much and describe things so well, such as your dance with Eva, but because of the discovery of what we have in common. A perfect' – he wheezed and gasped – 'perfect example of how the past is with us always. I should like to meet Michael. He is the security for both of us. To protect him, you will never talk. And I, knowing that, may rest easily. I would never tell him anything, of course. But still I wish to talk to him. Not that I would raise the question of his . . . paternity.' He almost whispered the last word, as if naming something sacred. 'Though I cannot help wondering about it. Who was his father – William? The unknown Russian soldier? Me? Probably you know, or at least have your own view, but nowadays there is DNA testing, so one could establish with certainty. If one wished.' As if at the thought, he shuddered and gasped again. 'My medicine, please.'

Edith froze inwardly, all her fears crystallized. The coldness that gripped her was not physical but an absolute zero of the spirit, a complete cutting-off. Her desire to protect her son from her own past was as all-consuming as her will to survive the bunker, but more ruthless. It filled her completely, too big for her to see. There was no space for the detachment that self-awareness demanded nor for an objective assessment of threat. She was her desire, her desire was her. She did not move.

His notebook and pencil slipped from his nerveless hands to the floor. His pale blue eyes clung to hers as he sank to his right until half out of the bed, his head hanging disconnectedly, his face bluish.

'My car, my medicine, my car . . .'

Edith did not move.

His eyes became paler and shallower, fish-like as they lost expression. His face continued to darken and his breath came in great straining convulsions that shook the bed. Edith felt them through the mattress. His blue and white striped pyjamas reminded her inconsequentially of the sofa on which Hitler and Eva died.

Eventually the slumped figure moved no more. The head lolled unpleasantly sideways, as if the neck were broken, threatening to topple the whole body out of bed. After waiting long enough to be sure, Edith rose and walked softly to the door. She would call the police first thing in the morning.

Then, when they had cleared the body away and done whatever was necessary, she would invite herself to lunch with Michael and Sarah and the children. She closed the door carefully behind her. Edith never looked back.

AFTERWORD

This story is a fiction: Eva Braun had no secretary. Anyone wanting to know what actually happened should read Hugh Trevor-Roper's *The Last Days of Hitler*, the first and still the most compelling account by an outsider of what happened in the bunker. Also, Traudl Junge's *Until the Final Hour*, the fullest and best insider's account both of the bunker and of life at the Berghof (the book on which the film *Downfall* was based). The National Archive at Kew has the MI5 file of contemporary interrogation reports on which Trevor-Roper drew for his book. For a fictional but factually based account of the Berghof, see Sibylle Knauss's novel *Eva's Cousin*.

There were historical originals for many of the scenes and events depicted or referred to here. One of the bunker secretaries (Martin Bormann's) really did marry her British army interrogator, as does Edith, and the cook, Constanze Manziarly, disappeared with two Russian soldiers in the way that Edith almost does, never to be seen again. The scene with the fortuitous corpse that saved Edith is based on an incident mentioned by Antony Beevor in his book *Berlin*.